The Diane Dimbleby Murder Collection

Murder Collection

Volume No. 1

Penelope Sotheby

Free Book

Sign up for this author's new release mailing list and receive a free copy of her very first novella _Murder At The Inn_. This fantastic whodunit will keep you guessing to the very end and is not currently available anywhere else.

Go to http://fantasticfiction.info/murder-at-the-inn/ to have a look.

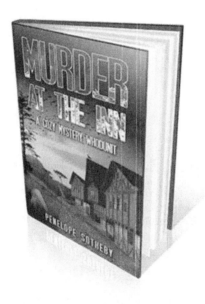

Other Books By The Author

Murder in Bermuda (Book 1 in the "Murder in Paradise" series)

Murder in the Bahamas (Book 2 in the "Murder in Paradise" series)

Murder in Jamaica (Book 3 in the "Murder in Paradise" series)

Murder in Barbados (Book 4 in the "Murder in Paradise" series)

Murder in Aruba (Book 5 in the "Murder in Paradise" series)

Murder at the Inn

Murder on the Village Green (A Diane Dimbleby Cozy Mystery)

Murder in the Neighbourhood (A Diane Dimbleby Cozy Mystery)

Murder on a Yacht (A Diane Dimbleby Cozy Mystery)

Murder in the Village (A Diane Dimbleby Cozy Mystery)

Murder in the Mail (A Diane Dimbleby Cozy Mystery)

Murder in the Hotel (A Daniel Swift Mystery)

Table of Contents

Murder on the Village Green

Chapter 1

Diane Dimbleby sits at her computer in her cozy cottage in Apple Mews, Shropshire. Taking a short break to stretch her wrists and relax her mind, she breathes in the fresh spring air coming in through the front window. She embraces the silence that is interrupted only slightly by the occasional song from a sparrow or chime from a pedal bike bell.

Closing her eyes, Diane goes back in time to Shrewsbury Abbey. That day she had headed to Shrewsbury to complete a self-guided tour of the town's historic buildings. She had completely researched and planned the itinerary herself.

She remembers seeing the crowd outside the main entrance of the abbey. Police constables were stationed between the group of people and the cordoned-off doorway. Diane smiles, remembering how she had somehow managed to sneak under the police tape to enter the church.

On her way to the Abbey, Diane had imagined she would be gazing in awe at its ornate stained glass and its original, nearly thousand-year-old columns. Instead, she was shocked to see smashed glass, punctured organ pipes, spilled hymnals and hacked pews. It was a ghastly sight.

Diane laughs at recalling how Inspector Darrell Crothers discovered that she was behind police lines inside the church.

Their paths had crossed many times throughout those days following the atrocious vandalism. Locals and so-called witnesses had immediately pointed the finger at a young chap, James Cooper. He was rough-around-the-edges and known for getting himself into trouble a handful of times. He was immediately pegged as the scoundrel responsible for the Abbey's destruction.

"The truth will set you free" is Diane's steadfast motto. She isn't so naïve to believe the justice system always embraces this philosophy. But she had shared this mantra with James Cooper when she had taken the liberty to question him the day after the vandalism.

Diane repeated this—"the truth will set you free"—to James because she wanted him to know that, if she had anything to do with it, his negative reputation would not impede a thorough investigation.

It was Diane's intuition and persistence that finally persuaded Inspector Crothers to consider another suspect. And she had been right. (She is all too often right, much to the dismay of Inspector Crothers, although he will eventually have to admit that she is a great help rather than a hindrance.)

It hadn't been James Cooper responsible for the vandalism. Rather, it had been a man who had reached breaking point, so to speak. He had recently been denied a recommendation from the Bishops' Advisory to pursue training towards becoming an ordained minister. The man had taken out his anger and self-loathing on one of Shrewsbury's most glorious buildings.

Diane snaps back to present day. Although less than an hour's drive, in some respects Shrewsbury feels like a world away from her little village of Apple Mews. And London feels like it's in a completely different galaxy.

Diane brings her fingers back to her keyboard and vividly describes the destruction she had witnessed inside Shrewsbury Abbey.

An hour of non-stop typing later, Diane stands and stretches to grasp her feet in a *Padahastana* position, her new favourite yoga pose. At 61 years old, she is the oldest in the village's yoga class—the class is probably the most avant-garde thing happening in Apple Mews at present. But Diane has no trouble keeping up with the participants who are 30 or more years her junior. Many of her classmates had been, at one time, her students.

Diane retired from teaching at the local school last year, and is now keeping plenty busy as an aspiring mystery novelist. Her stories are inspired by her own amateur detective experiences, like her time at

Shrewsbury Abbey. She likes to think her knack for solving crimes is a gift that was left to her by her late husband, David.

She had always admired David's profession—he had been a police inspector at Scotland Yard. Tragically though, he was killed in the line of duty when he was called to the scene of a robbery.

Diane and David had only been married for two years when he was killed. That was almost 30 years ago. It is still the largest loss and challenge she has experienced during her six decades on Earth.

"Well, I think I deserve a treat for finishing this chapter," says Diane out loud. "Maybe I'll go pick up the ingredients to bake some chocolate brownies!"

Grabbing her purse, Diane leaves her cottage without locking the door. Not once has she locked her door while living in Apple Mews.

She has lived most of her life in the Shropshire village, save for the couple of years in London with David. If she were back in London, she would surely lock the door, and maybe even install an alarm system. But not in Apple Mews.

Apple Mews is likely one of the most sober communities in the county. And that's just how Diane likes it. Besides, there is plenty to keep her entertained listening to the deliciously entertaining local gossip—there is no need for the hustle and bustle of city life.

On the way to the grocer, passing through the village green, Diane notices a man sitting on the plush grass. He is leaning against the sturdy trunk of an oak tree, reading a book. Diane does not recall ever meeting him before.

"Good afternoon!" she says in her customary manner.

Although some of the events that have come to characterize Diane's life would turn many of us sour, Diane is still as friendly to strangers as she is to long-time friends and neighbours.

The man does not look up. Diane suspects he is quite engrossed in his book. She won't bother disturbing him. She is hopeful that one day readers will be equally lost in one of her mystery stories.

Leisurely continuing through the green, Diane waves hello across the street to Gemma Evans. Gemma is watering the flowers outside the hotel she manages. Next door, the pub owner Alfie Parker is writing his 'Today's Specials' on the chalkboard sign.

Diane counts ten people—nine school children plus the local vicar, Reverend Harvey—lined up outside the café for Helen Bell's sticky buns, which are famous around the whole county.

When she reaches the local grocer, Diane is greeted by a colourful window display. Andrew Lloyd, the owner of the shop, prides himself on creating 'art' out of some of the merchandise he sells.

This particular version appears to be a tour route travelling to several of the region's villages. The 'map' is creatively illustrated by yellow beans, garlic scapes and aubergines. The tour bus looks to be painstakingly constructed out of a tea box and liquorice toffees.

Diane hears the ring of the familiar shopkeeper's bell as she walks through the front door.

"Good afternoon, Mrs. Dimbleby," says a burly, twinkle-eyed gent standing behind the counter. "Will you be joining the local produce tour this weekend? We have at least half a dozen farms arranged for the event. It shall be a delectable journey, oh a delectable journey!"

"I wouldn't miss it for the world, Andrew," says Diane, while endearingly reaching up to pick a yellow bean out of his full head of hair. "The roles are certainly reversed, aren't they? Instead of me quizzing you about the 100 Years' War, you are now my leading authority on all things fruit and veg."

"You were always my favourite teacher, Mrs. Dimbleby," says Andrew, blushing.

"And you were such a hard-working pupil."

Diane passes by tables filled with cauliflowers and lettuces, followed by cherries and strawberries, and heads to the baking aisle. She picks out a canister of cocoa and a bag of caster sugar.

"Baking brownies, I see. You must have finished the first five chapters?"

Diane turns around to see Albert and smiles.

Albert is Diane's dearest friend in Apple Mews (and possibly the closest of all the people she's called "friend" throughout her years). Their mutual affection for literature has tied them together for decades. More recently Albert has been the biggest supporter of Diane's writing.

"And you must be getting ready to tuck into Edward Rutherfurd's latest novel," says Diane, eyeing the baguette and Stilton cheese in his hands.

"Guilty," says Albert with his trademark silly smirk. "I'm also looking forward to tomorrow's edition of 'mead and mystery'."

Diane enjoys their regular meetings where Albert reads her latest chapters. They discuss what can be improved and what reads juicily well. These nights almost always involve a glass or two of spirits, hence the *mead* reference. Occasionally the time is complemented by a reading of one of the 'whodunit greats,' like Arthur

Conan Doyle or Agatha Christie, or even a viewing of an Alfred Hitchcock film.

"Tomorrow!" says Diane, her blue eyes beaming.

After paying for her ingredients, Diane leaves with a spirited pace, intent on smelling the aroma of baking brownies wafting through her cottage. She laughs as she dodges the primary students running down the lane with sticky buns in hand.

Returning through the village green, Diane sees more families and couples laying out picnic blankets to have their afternoon tea in the open air. A few adventurous souls in swimming costumes and trunks are testing the waters of the bordering lake. It will be at least a few more weeks before Apple Mews' main swimming and canoeing hole is swarming with locals and day-trippers.

It is such a lovely June day that Diane wonders whether sitting on the green reading a nice book might be more of a treat than chocolate brownies. Reading in a beautiful setting, just like the stranger she had noticed briefly before. *Is he still here?*

He is. Diane sees him leaning against the same tree, head bent towards the book still in his lap. She decides she'll go introduce herself, a fellow bibliophile, and find out which tome he is so captivated by.

As she approaches, Diane sees it is a slight breeze, not his fingers, turning the pages. Diane decides not to disturb his nap and turns away. But she is struck by how still he is, almost mannequin-like. Perhaps he is ill and needs help.

Diane turns back and slowly approaches the man. *Is his chest rising and falling?* She feels her stomach somersault as she nears the stranger. She drops her groceries and kneels to the ground.

"Are you quite alright, Sir?" she asks. "My name is Diane. Can you hear me?"

He still does not move.

She swallows hard, then discreetly moves her ear close to the man's nose and mouth and listens. She closes her eyes and concentrates, determined to hear even the smallest sign of air exchange.

But… she does not detect even a fraction of a breath.

Diane's wishes her instincts are wrong, but it appears they are correct. This stranger to Apple Mews is not sleeping, nor ill. He is dead.

Intent on remaining calm, Diane inhales and exhales deeply. There are families, some with young children, all across the green. Two parents and two tots have literally stretched out a picnic blanket only a handful of metres away. She must not provoke any sense of panic.

Covertly, she takes her cell phone out of her pocket. Turning away from the young family, she dials 999.

"999, what's your emergency?"

"I need you to send an ambulance and police assistance to the northeast quadrant of the common green on Main Street, Apple Mews. There is a deceased male, alone, leaning against a tree. Please hurry. There are many families in the park that could become frightened quite quickly once they get wind of this."

Diane hangs up the phone. How could she have not noticed someone dead, or in the process of dying, sooner? And so very close to home!

In the meantime, Diane concludes, it's best to clear vulnerable eyes from the area. She walks toward the family closest to the cadaver. She smiles gently at the two young children and approaches the dad.

"I don't want to alarm you," Diane whispers in the father's ear. "But the man behind me, leaning against that tree there, has passed away. I've called emergency services. I think it best that you move your sweet little dears down closer to the lake, away from the... *um*... action."

The father's eyes widen. "Oh my—!" he starts to gasp, but he is quickly shushed by his wife who grabs his arm firmly.

"Don't go all collywobbles on me Henry," his wife whispers harshly; and then, more jovially she says, "Come Tommy and Lucy... Dad will teach you how to skip rocks in the lake!"

Her husband does not follow right away, but instead gawks at the breathless man resting against the tree trunk. He covers his mouth as if he's about to be sick.

"Are you quite alright Sir?" asks Diane.

"I *said*... *Dad* will teach you how to skip rocks...HENRY!?! ... Lake! ... Now!" shouts the mom, rushing the children away.

Henry reluctantly obeys his wife, every so often turning back to stare at the lifeless body.

The sound of sirens can now be heard.

Main Street's tenants and purveyors begin to poke their heads out or come right outside to see what's happening. The sirens are a sound that is less than rarely heard in Apple Mews—as strange to the village as the dead man at the foot of the oak tree firmly rooted in the village green.

"Do you suppose someone has fallen ill at the nursing home, Gemma?" asks Alfie Parker outside his pub.

"Sounds like a whole cavalry of 'em, don't it?" says Gemma, equally bewildered.

A blue and yellow-chequered police car zooms down the road next to the green, followed by an ambulance. More villagers go outside their homes and businesses, scratching their heads.

Diane waves her arms like a crane engaged in a mating dance. The police officers and paramedics have no problem seeing the strikingly energetic, grey-haired woman flagging them down, and pull over.

Before the emergency personnel even exit their vehicles, rumours begin to spread amongst the amassing crowd.

Old Mr. Abrams has finally met his maker…

They're shooting a film all around Shrewsbury… they're making the clincher scene right here in our very own Apple Mews!

God love dear little Mrs. Jones. She's awfully sweet but too clumsy for her own good. What has she toppled into this time?

Diane quickly points the first responders towards the man who deserves their attention. One of the paramedics quickly confirms Diane's conclusion—the man, whoever he may be, is indeed dead.

"We're going to need the medical examiner and CID here," says one of the police constables over his radio.

The other constable begins to cordon off the area surrounding the oak tree and the deceased. At the same time, as he is setting up the yellow police tape, Diane does her best to usher the curious onlookers away from the scene.

"Do you want me to start collecting statements Constable?" asks Diane. "I'll go tell everyone who was here when the body was discovered to stay put until they are questioned. I think I can recall who's been here this whole time."

"That won't be necessary Mrs. Dimbleby," says a steady voice.

Standing just outside the cordoned-off scene is a plain clothes detective, in his mid-30s. Lean and muscular, the inspector's attractive features would be much more obvious if he would only crack a smile.

"Why if it isn't Inspector Darrell Crothers," says Diane, pleased.

Diane has always admired the inspector's sense of duty and justice. Although she thinks he still has lessons to learn as an investigator—he has trouble seeing the bigger picture sometimes—she knows they will come with age.

Sadly, Inspector Crothers does not feel the same way about seeing Diane. In fact, seeing the amateur sleuth, again, is making him feel a little shirty.

"We very much appreciate you calling the police Mrs. Dimbleby," says Inspector Crothers, gently pulling her a good distance away from the scene.

"Surely we're on a first-name basis by now, Darrell. Call me Diane," she grins. "How old are your dear children now?"

"We'll take it from here," says the inspector, ignoring her air of familiarity.

"But I need to tell you what I've observed. I saw the deceased leaning against the tree at least an hour ago on my way to the grocer's… and then I realized he was dead on the way back! And I just live right over there, almost directly across the way."

"And home is where you should be right now. You've had enough of a shock for one day. You need to leave it to the professionals now."

Inspector Crothers urges Diane to return to her cottage to have a nice cup of tea. Diane's stomach is grumbling, and she would really like to sit down to a cuppa, but she feels like she is a prime witness to at least this stage of the case.

If there is a case, that is. The man could have died of natural causes. But could this have possibly been a murder?

"Have you determined the cause of death?" asks Diane, a little less pleasantly this time.

Inspector Crothers picks up her groceries from the ground and asks a police constable to help her carry them to her cottage.

"Thank you for your time Mrs. Dimbleby… uh, thank you Diane," he says, trying to appease the wannabe detective.

"I'm going, I'm going," she says. "But I'll be expecting your call! I have an important statement to make."

Diane then thanks the constable but assures him she is quite capable of toting her groceries the *short distance* home.

Chapter 2

Diane slams the cupboard door after putting away the dry goods she bought earlier that afternoon. She is no longer in the mood to bake brownies. Not even the heavenly redolence of baking chocolate squares can cheer her up.

Surely Inspector Darrell Crothers knows he needs to ask Diane exactly what she saw. His constables are, at this very moment, taking witness statements from all the families and couples and friends who had been spending their time enjoying the lovely day on the green. Lovely day for all, except one poor gent.

He doesn't like an old biddy like me poking my nose into his investigation, thinks Diane. She has certainly helped the inspector close a case or two in the past though. Although he had never directly thanked her for her insight or for her clue detection talent, he has, at least unconsciously, understood that she is much more than a nosy busybody getting in the way of a criminal inquiry.

Diane sighs, her frustration beginning to wane. After all, she can certainly understand why Darrell, or any other detective for that matter, has to be cautious when it comes to civilians getting involved. *Just be patient Diane—he'll come around.*

She turns on the cooker, places the kettle on the front burner and drops a couple of teabags into her teapot. "A cup of tea would restore my normality," says Diane, quoting *Hitchhikers' Guide to the Galaxy*.

Feeling much calmer now, Diane sits at her desk in the front room. She looks out the window to see a uniformed officer questioning Henry, the husband and father who had been quite shaken up when he first realized there was a dead body in his midst. Now he appears much more at ease, even quite gallant, as he animatedly describes his account to the constable.

Diane stares at the mystery man, now a corpse, still leaning against the oak tree. She can see Darrell crouching down beside him; the inspector is staring at the man as if he is looking straight into his eyes. Except this man's eyes are closed up nice and tight.

The oak tree is directly across the street.

Diane had been at her desk writing most of the day. She hadn't noticed this stranger walk up to the tree or anybody else for that matter. *Did he walk there?* Diane shakes her head. If she had only looked up from her computer and turned her head slightly, she might have seen the poor fellow's arrival and even how he died.

But when Diane writes, nothing can drag her away from the scene she is describing, from the feelings and the grizzly details which she is imagining or recalling.

The kettle is whistling. Diane goes back to the kitchen and pours the boiling water inside her teapot. The steamy water becomes a tawny brown liquid. As the tea steeps, Diane traces the most pronounced wrinkle on her right hand, a habit of hers while in deep thought.

She tries to remember what *he* looked like. The man had been quite pale. And there had been something else—something that had caught her eye. Was it a dark spot on his shirt? Diane might have noticed such a spot, figuring it to be a stain from his lunch. But she couldn't be sure.

If she had seen a stain, could it have been blood? She still didn't know how he had died. Poor bloke could have died peacefully in his sleep. That wouldn't have been a bad way to go—curled up with a book, under a tree that had been there for many generations, on such a beautiful spring day.

Diane sits back at her desk with her cup of tea. Outside she sees two men in white crime scene suits carrying an elongated black bag. One is holding the head, the other the toe of the heavy duty duffel. *Will they be performing a post-mortem?*

Taking a sip of tea, Diane turns back to her computer. She opens a new Word document and types "June 2, 2015; 3:00pm," to start her witness statement for the police. She proceeds to describe the minute details of the afternoon, zeroing in on her observations of the gentleman in passing and up close.

Just as Diane is about to explain how she checked to see if the fellow had been breathing, the doorbell rings.

"I'll be right there Darrell," calls Diane, without looking up. She knew he was going to show up sometime before sunset.

Opening the door, Diane sees quite a different expression on Darrell's face: his facial appearance is part bashful, part nonchalant, rather than of a stern headmaster like when they conversed earlier in the day.

"How did you know it was me at the door?" asks Darrell.

Diane simply smiles and invites him in. "Would you like a cuppa? It is still hot."

Darrell nods his head and heads to the front window. His face breaks into a smile. He can clearly see the crime scene—the oak tree and its surroundings—directly from the front window of Diane's cottage.

Still smiling, he sits down on the sofa and accepts the cuppa from Diane.

"Just a little milk, if I remember correctly, Darrell?"

"Uh yes... thank you... Mrs... uh... Diane," he says gently.

Diane begins to see the inspector's true compassionate side again that devotion of his to protect society, and each individual victim, from the evils and horrors of this world.

Perhaps those evils or horrors have finally reached Apple Mews.

"Diane," Darrell continues. "Did you see anything out of the ordinary, anything at all, happen around the oak tree before you left your cottage this afternoon?"

"Sadly, no."

"Were you sitting there at all today?" the inspector asks, pointing at her desk with the computer sitting on top, along with pens and pencils, a notepad, her glasses and a thick volume titled *Oxford Dictionary of Law*.

"Yes, I was sitting there practically the whole day," says Diane.

"And you didn't see a thing?" Darrell asks, a slight irritation permeating his tone.

That didn't last long, thinks Diane regarding his amiable nature.

"If I sat there staring out the window all the time, of course I would have seen something, and probably something crucial," she says. "But I rarely sit there to watch people. I'm there working and writing my novel...

"... And when I'm writing, I'm transported to the very scene that I'm describing," Diane muses. "Sometimes it feels like I'm not here at all when I'm deep in one of my writing sessions."

"Uh huh," says Darrell, not quite certain he understands, but confident Diane is telling the truth.

"And," the inspector continues, "did you recognize the man when you approached him?"

"I have never laid eyes on him before, poor bloke," Diane says, shaking her head, eyes down.

"And to your knowledge, does the name Paul Tucker ring any bells?"

Diane thinks back to the vast number of people she's met throughout her life: David's colleagues in London, her friends and cousins now living near and far, the people she's met through travels and the cultural activities and volunteering she's done all around the county, the decades of students she taught...

"I can't say I've ever met a Paul Tucker," she says. "Is that who—"

"Well, I must be off. Thanks so much for the cuppa," interjects Darrell.

The inspector carefully places the English bone china cup on the coffee table and starts to stand.

"Wait!" shouts Diane, startling the inspector into sitting again. "Just two shakes of a lamb's tail!"

She runs back to her computer and begins typing again at top speed.

Darrell sits back down. His eyes wander back to the teacup. He hadn't noticed before, but the cup and saucer had an unusual pattern—not of roses or lilacs, but of round-leaved sundew.

The round-leaved sundew—*Drosera rotundifolia.* The inspector is quite adept at identifying local plant species, as well as bird songs and animal tracks. He had grown up spending practically all of his waking hours outside, and he adored the countryside. His father had been a farmer and Darrell had nearly followed in his footsteps. But fate had other ideas…

Even though the round-leaved sundew is Shropshire's county flower, the red, hairy leaves seem a strange theme for a teacup, as does the plant's carnivorous nature.

I will catch the killer, just like the sundew catches insects.

The inspector's daydreaming is interrupted by the sound of Diane's printer. She removes two sheets from the dispenser tray and passes it to Darrell.

"My official witness statement," says Diane.

"Thanks again for the cuppa," he says, folding the statement and placing it in his suit jacket pocket.

Walking towards his second-hand Range Rover, Darrell sees that the village green is eerily abandoned, save for the yellow police tape surrounding the old oak tree. A few villagers are still congregated outside their homes in whispers, wondering who the strange man is and how he died.

Before Darrell starts the engine of his Range Rover, he rings his wife, Claire. He lets her know not to wait for him for dinner, but that he'll be home in time to read goodnight stories to their little ones.

Darrell doesn't like to miss family dinners—and he makes an effort to be home for these more often than not—but this evening he has to go back the Shrewsbury Police Station and meet with the medical examiner.

The inspector slowly drives by the villagers still outside, nodding his head. They gaze back with curious, or perhaps fearful, expressions.

Is our village no longer safe?

Over the metal bridge crossing the river, and around two bends, and Darrell is once again driving on the trunk road back to Shrewsbury. If he had been with Claire and their children Jeremy and Chloe, he would have enjoyed taking them on the scenic drive. But he has to take the quickest route today—he doesn't like to waste time when he's on a case.

Of course most people, except for a few of his colleagues, don't know there is, in fact, a case—a case of murder. Not even Diane knows yet, although Darrell suspects her instincts are telling her there is a criminal element to the man's fateful demise.

Based on their conversation, Darrell has established that Diane has never seen the victim, Paul Tucker, before today, and that she does not remember knowing anybody with that name.

Darrell had found a wallet in the victim's pocket—presumably it belonged to him. Inside the wallet, he had found a driver's license belonging to a Paul Tucker who had a Sheffield address. The license picture looked a lot like the victim, although it is sometimes difficult to tell accurately when one's eyes are shut and skin is pale.

Although Diane had seen Mr. Tucker leaning against the tree on her way to the grocer, and then again upon returning home when she discovered that he was dead, she has no idea how or why he happened to be sitting under the oak tree. She has no idea *yet*…

My instincts tell me that I'll need Diane's help with this case too. Darrell shakes his head, half annoyed, half charmed.

Upon arriving at the police station, he immediately sees Dr. William Jackson waiting for him in the entryway. He sees that look in the medical examiner's eyes—a look he's seen only seen a couple of times. It's a look that means this is no ordinary case.

"I think you'd better come down to the lab with me," says Dr. Jackson.

Darrell, as fit as he is, practically has to jog to keep up with the pathologist's pace.

"What's going on William?" asks the inspector.

"Looking at the victim on the scene on the village green, I had my suspicions," says the medical examiner. "But I couldn't be sure until I brought him back to the lab."

The sterile white walls of the corridor lead them into the equally sterile white-walled autopsy room. The lab is lit by invasively bright fluorescent lights. The smell of formaldehyde enters Darrell's nostrils as they pass by two empty silver autopsy tables to reach the last one where Paul Tucker is lying.

The victim is lying on his back and his clothes have been removed. Darrell looks down to see several lacerations across his torso. The majority are roughly sewn or stapled shut, except for one.

Darrell is speechless, staring at the long, deep gash that is only partially sealed. The skin surrounding the laceration is blood-stained. Slippery structures that only an anatomical expert could name precisely can be seen with a quick glance through the open cavity.

"So is the cause of death exsanguination?" Darrell asks. It is quite obvious a person could bleed to death from such a gouge. "And that means he did not die where Diane... *er,* Mrs. Dimbleby found him because there are no significant blood pools at the scene."

"Yes, you are correct, but that's not all," says Dr. Jackson. "I've performed an ultrasound on him to be certain. I did not want to reopen the incisions until you saw them first. His kidneys and liver are missing."

"Crikey!" shouts Darrell. "And based on these gashes and staples and things, by missing, we're probably assuming stolen!?!"

"Rightly so," says Dr. Jackson. "It looks like the organ thieves tried to close up all of the incisions, but poor Mr. Tucker bled out before they finished suturing."

Darrell is simply disgusted. In the 15 or so years he's served as a copper and risen up the ranks from Trainee Investigator to Detective Inspector, he's seen an awful lot. He's dealt with addicts who have overdosed on the streets or in their depressing one-room homes shared with other junkies. He's been the lead detective in cases of brutal stabbings, shootings, murder-suicides... he's even had his heart broken a number of times dealing with domestic abuse cases—the hardest times have been when children are involved.

He had also been the main witness to a fatal hit-and-run, back when he was in high school. Except that was personal. His best friend had been the victim. It was the reason why Darrell joined the police force; why he decided not to become a farmer like his father.

And to this day, investigators have not—*he has not*—found the driver responsible for killing his best mate. Darrell can still see, clear to this day, the car slam into Peter. He remembers the sound of the impact of the vehicle striking against the flesh and bones of his innocent friend. And then he remembers running up to Peter lying on the ground, and his friend is so quiet, so still...

Yes, Darrell has seen a lot in his 36 years of life. But illegal organ harvesting? This is a first for him. He had wondered whether organ theft was even real or an urban legend instead. But here it is, a case right here in the county of Shropshire, and the body was found in the one of the safest villages in the country, Apple Mews!

"Nobody... *nobody*... deserves to die like this," says Darrell.

"Has anyone spoken to his next-of-kin?" asks Dr. Jackson.

"We have someone from the Sheffield police driving a Mrs. Tucker here right now," says Darrell solemnly. "She's coming to confirm the victim's identity."

The next morning Diane is up even earlier than usual. A cup of tea in hand, she stares outside her window instead of at her computer screen. Although she had planned to write at least another chapter today, she is finding it quite difficult to concentrate.

A whole chorus of songbirds are singing in Diane's garden and in the village green across the way. Their morning melodies are forever consistent—they are not cancelled on holidays or for "moments of silence" when somebody dies, even if the dearly departed had been "resting peacefully" against one of their favourite perching places not even 24 hours ago.

After her tea, hardly touched, turns much too cold to enjoy, Diane sees children in uniforms running towards the primary school. For a moment the retired schoolteacher is swept back to the times where she drank up the enthusiasm of her former students. She had been a favourite for many of them; they never dreaded coming to her classes, although Diane is much too modest to admit this.

Diane sees a police car pull up and park next to the green. A constable gets out and walks towards the crime scene. It only takes him a couple of minutes to remove the yellow police tape, get back in his car and drive away.

That's strange, thinks Diane. The police tape has been taken down already. She's quite sure no forensic team personnel had analysed the scene. And she has been at her window from the time Inspector Darrell Crothers left until nightfall yesterday, and then again early this morning.

Perhaps they did not need to perform any forensic sweeps because the man had died of natural causes. Or he had died of suspicious circumstances, but someplace else and the oak tree is merely the dump site.

Diane decides she'll do a little forensic investigating of her own… just in case something was missed. She grabs her notebook, hangs her camera around her neck and puts on her glasses.

She walks across the street at a brisk pace, looking over her shoulder several times. Before entering what had been the cordoned-off crime scene, she pulls out a pair of gloves and booties and puts them on her hands and feet. She often carries a pair of each on her person, knowing that one never knows when one might stumble upon the scene of a crime.

Diane walks concentrically around the oak tree, slowly moving closer and closer to the where she had found the man the day prior. She stops suddenly, crouches down, and picks a four-leaf clover. She has a knack for spotting them from feet away.

She continues inspecting the scene with a fine-toothed comb. She stops and takes several pictures of the grass the mystery man had been sitting on top of yesterday, before jotting something down in her book. She then takes a photo of the bark at the base of the tree trunk and writes another note.

She crouches down and walks slowly around the tree without breaking her squat-pose. She sees something sticking out of the dirt, so uses her gloved fingers to dig and uncover the item. She manages to pry the item from the grips of the ground and continues crouching and moving around the trunk.

In the corner of her eyes, Diane sees something *or someone* moving slowly behind her. A flurry of thoughts fills her mind.

What if the mystery man had indeed been murdered?

And his killer is back…

And I'm going to be the next victim…

Diane quietly gulps. She tries to remember some of the moves she had learned at a self-defence class she had taken right after David was killed back in London. But that had been nearly 30 years ago.

Was there a backwards kick or elbow move she had practiced? There is no time to think. Diane instead decides she better hop as far ahead as she can and then break into a run. She bends and springs her knees, frog-like, and leaps one metre forward. Not bad!

But her curiosity prevents her from continuing her escape. She turns around, hoping to get a good look of the potential suspect.

She turns around quickly and is surprised to see Inspector Darrell Crothers crouching, just like she had been, beside the tree.

"What are you doing here?!?" they both yell at the same time.

Diane quickly hides the item she had dug up behind her back.

Chapter 3

Darrell hadn't slept well last night.

After reading Jeremy and Chloe their stories and tucking them into bed, he told Claire he was just going to do some case research—"just for a half hour"—before tucking himself into bed next to her. Thirty minutes turned to surfing on the Internet until the wee hours of the morning.

An increased demand in people waiting for organ transplant, a decreased supply of donors desperate to earn cash or fooled into having a "necessary operation" and their organs are unknowingly removed or victims kidnapped and coerced to part with a body part.

Darrell read through a series of these traumatic cases, like that of the British student found in a flat in Belgrade. At first Serbian authorities deemed the cause of death to be a heroin overdose, but it was later found out that his heart and pancreas had been extracted.

Darrell also learned that the World Health Organization had estimated that around the world, every hour more than one illegal kidney operation takes place. More than one an hour! But surely this was more a problem in India, Pakistan, China, Brazil... not in England!

Yet Darrell had read about how in 2012, it was revealed that a British crime firm had cunningly lured a woman to the UK to harvest her organs. Although it is not clear whether organs were stolen, it was allegedly the first case of human trafficking for the purpose of illegal organ harvesting ever reported in the UK.

And now here is Paul Tucker, discovered in Darrell's policing area, apparently robbed of his kidneys and liver. Had he been captured or duped? Or had he even willingly agreed to be a living donor, perhaps agreeing to give away just one of his kidneys in exchange for a hefty sum, but then exploited for more than he had consented to?

Desperate financial times called for desperate measures. Likewise, greed could propagate horrific acts.

When Darrell finally went to bed and cycled into REM sleep, he had some horrifically strange dreams. He could only recall snapshots: *a corroded scalpel... a bloody sheet... a victim waking up during "surgery"... an innocent child coaxed to follow a stranger...*

So when Darrell woke up this morning, he was zonked. And when Darrell is exhausted, he can be quite giddy, or silly really, no matter the reason for being so tired.

Thus upon discovering Diane crouched beside the oak tree in Apple Mews' green, Darrell's first reaction is not of dismay, but of whimsy. He decides to crouch behind her to see how long it takes this sweet, older, but still spry woman to notice his presence.

When Diane lunges forward and turns to face him, Darrell cracks up laughing with, surprisingly frolicsome enthusiasm. His laughter is so amusing that Diane cannot remain irritated from being so startled. She stands up laughing too, shaking her head in amusement.

Again, they ask at the same time, "What are you doing here!?!"

"It's obvious why I'm here, isn't it?" says Darrell, still chuckling. "I'm investigating a…"

Darrell realizes he has almost said too much.

"Investigating a murder, perhaps?" asks Diane, grinning inquisitively.

Darrell turns around and takes several steps away before asking, "So have you found anything interesting?"

Diane walks to the side of the tree where the mystery man had been sitting. She points to the base of the oak and looks at Darrell. He comes closer to inspect and sees what Diane is pointing to on the tree bark.

"Traces of blood," he says, taking out his phone to snap a picture.

"No need, Darrell," Diane says, pointing to the camera around her neck. "I'd be happy to print all of the pictures I took for you."

"You don't faff about, do you Diane," Darrell says, snapping a few photos just the same.

Diane states that the traces on the bark seem to be the only blood in the vicinity.

"If he had died from a wound of any sort, he would have bled on the ground until his heart stopped," she continues. "But if that were the case we would have found a big, blood pool stain here. I know my eyes are not what they used to be, but it's clear there is no such stain present… and it has not rained since three days ago, which is long before the body was deposited here."

"Deposited, you say," says Darrell, playfully mimicking curiosity.

"Yes, deposited!" Diane confidently says. "Because he must have died somewhere else, the place where he bled out. He was simply brought here post-mortem."

Diane does not stop there with her deductions. Taking in a deep breath, she exhales into an interpretation of the patch of grass, clearly matted, where the man had been sitting yesterday. "His body must have been placed here hours before I noticed him on my way to the grocer. It was probably brought here quite early in the morning before anybody was out and about."

"Those are some interesting theories," says Darrell, not completely letting on that every morsel from her mouth is a credible conclusion he agrees with.

"Oh, and I found something," says Diane, revealing what she is hiding behind her back—the object she had found at the base of the tree. It is a green piece of plastic the same size and shape as a business card.

"It looks like a hotel keycard," says Darrell, his tone more serious now. This piece of evidence is a complete surprise to him. How could he have missed it yesterday?

Diane nods her head in agreement. She traces her finger along the letters inscribed on the card—a cursive FR. "A hotel with FR as its initials perhaps," she contemplates out loud.

"The Footmen Rooming House... no... the Friendly Roadhouse... no, of course not," ponders Darrell.

"I wonder if it's the Farmer's Refuge Inn," says Diane, unsure of her guess.

Darrell quickly looks Diane straight in the eyes.

"Well, I must take my leave now Inspector," Diane then announces. "You don't want me mucking about your investigation. Besides, I have things I need to tend to other than searching for clues all day."

Diane gives Darrell a wink and walks towards her cottage without saying another word.

"The Farmer's Refuge Inn," Darrell whispers to himself. "I think she's right!"

Inside her cottage, Diane inches her way slowly towards the front window so as to not be seen. Hiding behind the batik curtain, Diane peeks to see Darrell continuing to survey the oak tree and the ground and grass surrounding it. He appears to scan much slower this time. Perhaps he's worried he'll miss another vital clue, although Diane had noticed he looks particularly exhausted today.

Darrell looks up towards Diane's cottage. Diane quickly drops to the ground for fear of being caught snooping. She manages not to be detected by the detective, but in doing so knocks over a stack of books along with a spider plant and the end table it was sitting upon.

Removing the dangling spider plantlets out of her grey hair, she slowly rises so her blue eyes are just barely able to spy through the bottom of the window. Diane sees Darrell walking towards his Range Rover.

Diane stands up completely, now feeling the effects of her 'graceful' crash to the floor. She repositions the books, stands up the table and places the spider plant back on top, lovingly patting its soil to ensure it is still firmly rooted, just like the old oak tree outside her window.

Diane lays out her yoga mat to stretch out her aching knees and shins. She cannot afford to sustain any serious injuries, not when Darrell would be needing her help on this case. He must be on his way to the Farmer's Refuge Inn, she thinks. She better get her case notes organized and then get some of her own writing done before Darrell comes back, Diane thinks with foresight.

Feeling much more limber, she sits at her desk and types the notes she recorded from the scene around the oak tree. She prints the document and inserts it into a new file folder. She then removes the memory card from her camera and inserts it into the computer drive. While the pictures are printing, Diane sticks a white label on the file folder—her "case file". After a little mulling over, she decides to call the folder "Murder on the Green."

Although Inspector Darrell Crothers did not yet reveal that the mystery man had been murdered, Diane is quite certain he was. Or at least his death was suspicious. After all, Diane is quite certain he was already dead when moved to the village green. That seems suspicious in itself—being moved to a public park after one's died—she thinks.

Diane realizes she must try to forget about this particular case at hand temporarily, and, for at least a couple of hours, revisit the vandalism at Shrewsbury Abby—the case inspiring the detective novel she is working on.

She looks up at a quotation card that she's pasted on the wall in front of her—*"Procrastination is the thief of time, collar him ~ Charles Dickens"*—and starts typing.

Darrell parks his Range Rover across from the Farmer's Refuge Inn. He crosses the medievalesque road to the lodging house whose timber Tudor-style and black and white aesthetic matches a number of the buildings in the area.

"I'd like to speak to the manager," says Darrell to the young man standing behind the Farmer's Refuge front desk.

"He told me he shan't be disturbed under any circumstances," replies the clerk, slightly nervous. "He said I should only fetch him if a Miss Shepherd arrives…

I think he must fancy her," the clerk adds, whispering this time.

"Why don't you let me go fetch the manager," says Darrell, flashing his badge along with a confident grin. "You just point the way and let me take care of the rest."

The clerk lets out a nervous chuckle and points to the closed door behind him. "I'm going to go take my 15-minute break," he says, walking away expeditiously.

Darrell holds his breath to refrain from bursting out in laughter and knocks on the manager's door.

"Bloody hell Dylan, didn't I tell you to leave me be?" shouts the manager from behind the door.

Darrell knocks again.

"SHOVE OFF!" yells the manager, swinging open the door. Within less than a second, the manager's face transforms from anger to fear. Only reaching Darrell's shoulders, the manager immediately eyes the detective inspector badge.

"I cannot shove off just yet," says Darrell, attempting to maintain a straight face, still feeling the giddy effects of his exhaustion. "I'm Inspector Detective Darrell Crothers. I'd like to ask a few questions."

"Oh, sorry about that mate," says the manager. "The name's Silas Crocker. Sorry about the cock up there.

That Dylan is a bit daft if you ask me. He is constantly asking questions about this and that. I thought it was him knocking, wanting to bother me again."

"And you are the manager of the Farmer's Refuge?"

"That I am. What brings you here?"

Darrell pulls out the green keycard that Diane found earlier this morning. "Is this one of your property's room keycards?"

Silas Crocker nods his head.

"I don't suppose you can tell me which room this might belong to?"

"Inspector, I'd like to help you out, really I would, but we're a respectful business here, that we are. We make sure things are confidential-like for our guests."

"I think if you match this keycard to the name in your register, you'll find the name Paul Tucker. And if that's the case, Paul Tucker is now the subject of an inquiry."

Of course, Darrell cannot be certain the keycard belongs to Paul Tucker. For all he knows, it could have been dropped on the green ages ago. But perhaps Diane's sleuthing would bring him luck once again.

Silas begrudgingly goes out to the front desk and swipes the keycard through a machine connected to the inn's main computer. In a few moments, Darrell can see for himself a record of Paul Tucker's booking in the system: he checked in on May 30th and is scheduled to check out on June 6th, three days from now.

"Do you remember anything about this guest?" asks Darrell.

Silas thinks for a moment, appearing as though he's concentrating quite intensively. "If I can remember nicely, I think he was travelling alone. Yes, that's right, because I remember him talking to a real gorgeous bird. She looked real fit you know, and she had this beautiful long, black hair."

"And?" says Darrell, interrupting the manager's state of reverie.

"I remember asking him, Mr. Tucker, if that fine-looking woman was his wife. He says no, he was travelling alone. What a shame."

"Is there anything else you can remember?"

Silas thinks once more and chuckles. "He asked me directions to Pontesbury. He wanted to see an old house there that he heard was haunted. He fancied himself to be a ghost hunter I expect."

Darrell jots some things down in his notebook. "Well, I'm going to have to examine his room."

Before Silas can object, Darrell smoothly snags the keycard from the manager's hand. There is no need for him to inquire about the room number. He can see for himself on the computer screen that Paul Tucker had been staying in room 13.

Expectantly, a DO NOT DISTURB sign is hanging outside on the doorknob of Paul Tucker's room. Darrell puts on a pair of gloves, swipes the card through the keycard lock and slowly enters the room.

Immediately Darrell smells a foul odour, a combination of must and soiled clothing. He switches on the light. The room is a real dog's dinner, but at first glance, it appears more like a bachelor pad than a murder scene.

On the table, Darrell notices several books on sightseeing in Shropshire and also on local ghost tales. Interestingly the bed is stripped, and the linen does not appear to be any place in the room.

Then Darrell notices that the lampshade on the bedside table has an odd shape. He moves closer to see it is not the lamp shade's natural shape; instead, it looks like it's been dented or jabbed. *Possible sign of a struggle?*

On the other side of the bed, Darrell sees a dark stain on the floor that has a diameter of approximately 30 centimetres. He's seen this shade of stain before. He's almost certain it's blood.

Inside the bathroom, he notes several dried blood droplets in the sink. In the bathtub, there are four ice buckets along with a mound of soiled towels.

This has got to be the actual scene of the crime—the place where those monsters stole poor Mr. Tucker's organs. Darrell calls into the station to request that the forensic scene investigation team come to the Farmer's Refuge immediately.

Darrell has to speak to Paul Tucker's wife as soon as possible. He heads to the police station, once the forensics investigators have arrived, to see if she is still there.

When he arrives, he finds Mrs. Tucker with the police chaplain. She is sipping slowly from a Styrofoam cup and staring blankly at the floor while the chaplain is talking softly beside her.

Darrell makes eye contact with the chaplain who nods. The chaplain places his hand on Mrs. Tucker's shoulder and makes his retreat. Darrell sits down next to the shocked wife.

"Mrs. Tucker," says Darrell gently. "I'm so sorry for your loss."

Mrs. Tucker does not even blink.

"Mrs. Tucker, I'm so sorry to disturb you right now, but I need your help. I need to ask you a few questions about your husband. Is that ok?"

This time, Mrs. Tucker slightly nods her head.

"You live in Sheffield?"

"Yes," she says softly.

"And so did your husband?"

Mrs. Tucker nods her head, just barely refraining from sobbing.

"And do you know why he was staying at an inn, the Farmer's Refuge, here in Shrewsbury?" Darrell asks delicately.

"He was here for his ghost research," she says. "He would go twice a year, to a different county each time. This trip was to explore Shropshire. To visit the places he read about in ghost story books. He is fascinated by ghosts... he *was* fascinated by ghosts."

Mrs. Tucker stops, swallowing hard.

"And when was the last time you spoke to your husband?"

"Right before he left," she smiles for the first time. "I like to give him his space for these trips. Just like he gives me my space for my spa days with the girls. We trust each other… *trusted* each other."

Mrs. Tucker starts tearing up again.

"Do you have some family coming to be with you?" asks Darrell.

"Yes, my brother and his wife will be here soon."

Darrell thanks Mrs. Tucker for her time.

The DO NOT DISTURB sign and the fact that Paul Tucker's wife did not expect to hear from him until he returned to Sheffield explained why no alarm bells had been sounded about the state of his room or his being. But how did the person or persons who performed the fatal organ harvest gain access to his hotel room?

Darrell decides he had better go visit Diane. He needs to tell her that the hotel keycard she found is proving very helpful to the murder inquiry. What Darrell cannot quite admit is that he needs Diane's insight to help him interpret the observations and theories scurrying around his pounding head.

When Darrell is at the door of Diane's house, it's nearly lunchtime.

Diane opens her front door and invites him in. Darrell walks in to see a small dining table set for two. The salmon on toasts, the fresh green drizzled with raspberry vinaigrette and sparkling mineral water make Darrell's stomach growl. He realizes he hasn't consumed anything yet today except for several cups of coffee—something he only drinks when he's knackered.

"Oh, I'm terribly sorry to interrupt," says Darrell, about to take his leave. "I can see you are expecting company for lunch."

"I am," says Diane. "A very important guest, as a matter of fact."

Chapter 4

Darrell is disappointed. He really wanted to tell Diane that the hotel keycard is proving to be a valuable piece of evidence.

He could also really use the clarity she tends to generate… and perhaps he is, in this single moment, also desperate for the comfort someone of her age and disposition provides.

"I won't take up any of your time then," says Darrell, trying to mask his chap-fallen sentiments. "Perhaps I can drop by later this afternoon…"

Diane breaks into exuberant laughter—this particular laugh of hers is *almost* always contagious—causing Darrell to turn red.

"Come through you silly goose! It is you I'm expecting for lunch."

"Well, that's just fine then. I was starting to drool over your spread," Darrell chuckles, attempting to be more light-hearted.

After Diane tells the inspector to stop fussing and to join her at the table, Darrell takes a bite of salmon toast. This, he realizes, is what his churning and fretful stomach has been missing all day. It is a welcome sensation, especially after the night he had. For the first time since learning that poor Paul Tucker's kidneys and liver were stolen, Darrell is able to relax, and even feel some ounce of hope that the organ ring killers will be apprehended.

"I thank you Diane, this meal is hitting the spot."

"You're quite welcome Darrell… but I expect you did not come here simply to discuss my culinary abilities."

Darrell clears his throat and contemplates what he will say next. He takes another bite of salad, a sip of mineral water and waits until his mouth is completely empty.

"It turns out the green card you found is indeed a hotel keycard. And you were right to guess it belongs to the Farmer's Refuge Inn."

Diane eyes Darrell, expectantly sensing he has more to share.

"And we've determined that the keycard is a vital clue to this particular investigation," Darrell says, being very careful not to reveal more than he should.

Diane only takes but a brief moment to enjoy the satisfaction that she had found something significant to help with the case. Her delight, however, quickly changes to inquisitiveness.

"Can you now tell me how *Paul Tucker* died?" asks Diane.

Diane has easily figured out the name of the victim! Darrell does not know if he should be surprised or impressed. Then again he had asked her, just the day before, whether she was familiar with the name.

Darrell folds his napkin as compactly as the piece of linen will allow. He normally cannot discuss an open case with a material witness. Yet from their past dealings, he knows he can trust Diane. And if he is completely honest with himself, Darrell knows Diane's beneficial assistance will likely go beyond that of her initial statement. It already has.

"I'm willing to provide you with answers to *some* of your questions," Darrell says, "but only if you promise to keep whatever I tell you under your hat."

"Of course I will! This is not my first criminal investigation, as you know. Who am I going to tell anyway?" asserts Diane, although her mind drifts to Albert. She finds it hard to keep anything from him— especially anything as fascinating as a possible murder inquiry. But it will have to be mum's the word, even while speaking with her close friend.

Darrell takes one last bite of salmon toast and wipes his mouth with his tightly folded napkin. Drawing in a big breath, he says, "You asked how Paul Tucker died. It was murder, but perhaps a murder that even you, Mrs. Dimbleby... Diane... have not even guessed. Dr. Jackson, the medical examiner, determined that the cause of death was exsanguination. That means—"

"A fatal form of blood loss," Diane jumps in.

"Yes, you're right," says Darrell. "And, specifically, Mr. Tucker bled out after his kidneys and liver were removed. We are quite certain he is the victim of illegal organ harvesting."

Diane gasps and covers her mouth for a long time. She is completely shocked. Like Darrell, she has come across or heard about a significant number of gruesome crimes, but none like this. Harvesting one's organs against one's will or without one's knowledge has got to be one of the cruellest crimes in existence.

She had done quite a bit of research on organ trafficking. *What was it that provoked that?* Oh yes, it was that time when she and Albert had watched *Dirty Pretty Things*. Albert had wanted to watch the film for some time because of its impressive wins at the British Independent Film Awards back in 2003. Diane remembers Albert had been worried the film's title would embarrass her. "Pshaw," she had said, urging him to start playing the movie.

Dirty Pretty Things had opened Diane's eyes to the gruesome trade of desperate persons giving up their kidneys in exchange for falsified travel documents. When she started researching the topic, it did not appear that illegal organ harvesting was actually a problem specific to London or any place in the UK. But Diane did glean a global overview of the atrocious trade.

She learned that kidneys are the most common among illegally harvested organs. Kidneys seem to be highest in demand and perhaps they are the cheapest to acquire; not to mention the fact that individuals can still live quite healthily after losing one of their two kidneys— although traffickers might not give a damn about their "organ donors'" quality of life afterwards.

Diane also knows that victims are generally alive when organs are harvested. If the operation is performed by a licensed surgeon, and the victim is under anaesthesia, there is a chance of survival. But if the operation is performed shoddily by an unqualified quack, death is almost a certainty.

"Death is almost a certainty," Diane ruminates out loud.

"Sorry?" asks Darrell gently.

Diane shakes her head—she had simply been talking to herself. She continues shaking her head over the severity of Paul Tucker's murder.

"Diane, the keycard you found next to the oak tree... it was the keycard to Paul Tucker's room at the Farmer's Refuge."

Darrell continues describing the hotel room: the missing bed linen, the pile of towels in the bathroom, the ice buckets, the large stain on the floor, the dented lampshade.

"Do you think then, that Mr. Tucker's organs were extracted... stolen... in his hotel room?" asks Diane.

"Yes, we are treating his room at the Farmer's Refuge as the actual scene of the crime," says Darrell, walking towards Diane's front window. "And the oak tree is the disposal site."

Darrell and Diane say their goodbyes, giving each other knowing glances. They are both quite certain they will see each other again during the course of this investigation.

Diane sits at her desk still feeling astonished by what she has just learned. The very act of having a part so internal removed—literally from inside one's body— would probably make many of us feel somewhat vulnerable, even if it is a procedure deemed medically necessary like the blissful occasion of the birth of a child.

Thus, the idea of some part being ripped from inside a person without their consent, or through sheer force, is so heinous... so violating... almost personal.

But the truth is, those who killed Paul Tucker probably did not know him from Adam. They probably targeted him within a short span of time, identifying some gullible or over-trusting aspect of his demeanour. Or perhaps it was even a blitz attack.

The motive for this despicable crime is probably one that has persisted throughout the ages: greed. Diane remembers, more recently, reading a newspaper article about brokers selling kidneys to wealthy patients for $200,000 American, and a heart for a colossal one million dollars!

If Diane can do anything to stop these money-hungry, despicable individuals from stealing any more organs, she will.

She wonders if there is any more evidence still hidden around the oak tree. She had not spent much time there investigating before Darrell arrived this morning. Plus, the green keycard she had found had blended in with its surroundings and was partially covered by dirt. Maybe there are more clues that require some prolonged and careful searching in order to be found.

Then again, the keycard was only *half* buried. Is it possible that one of the accomplices that had participated in the loathsome act had planted the card there purposefully? Maybe he or she had been forced into this awful scheme. Maybe the so-called accomplice deems the nature of the crime to be as vile as Diane and Darrell think it is and wants the police to catch the traffickers before they can strike again.

Without taking any more time to deliberate, Diane decides she must go back to the disposal site to see if she can find more clues left behind, by accident or design. She quickly opens the front door and sees Albert facing her, holding a pan of brownies.

Diane stops herself from shrieking. Albert is the last person that would instil fear into the retired schoolteacher, but her purpose-driven brain and adrenaline-filled body had not been expecting to see anybody standing in front of her cottage at this very moment.

"I brought brownies," says Albert, matter-of-factly, walking past Diane to her kitchen.

"Thank you," Diane says, not sure whether to be annoyed that her mission has been interrupted or touched by Albert's thoughtfulness.

"I figured you were probably not in the mood to bake brownies. I heard it was you that found the mysterious body yesterday," he says, giving her a look of concern, rather than one of a meddler.

Diane relaxes and cuts them each a brownie. She does not invite him to sit and stay a while, however.

Leaning against the kitchen counter, Diane closes her eyes and bites into the chocolate square.

"Mmmmm," she utters sincerely. "Albert, you never cease to amaze me. I've always known you are a wonderful chef, but now I can add baking to your long list of talents."

"Thank you Diane. But are you quite alright? I mean with what happened yesterday?"

"Of course I am! You know me, I've observed—and written about—much worse," Diane winks.

Oh, how Diane wishes to elaborate and tell Albert all about the clues she's found, and what she now knows must have happened in a hotel room in Shrewsbury. But she has made Inspector Darrell Crothers a promise and she shall keep it.

Diane gently ushers Albert back to the front door telling him that she is in the midst of a particularly productive writing session, and she does not wish to break the creative flow. Is it wrong to tell a fib to your best friend, she wonders?

"I shall see you tonight at yours, for mead and mystery!" she adds, promptly shutting the door.

How on Earth will I get through the evening with Albert without revealing any of the inquiry's pertinent details?

Diane peeks out the front window to watch Albert walk, rather hesitantly, away. After he changes his mind not once, but twice, to walk straight back to Diane's front door before deciding against it, he finally walks out of view. To be sure, Diane waits for her cuckoo clock's minute hand to shift three places before heading outside.

Before her right foot steps onto the village green, Diane hears her name being called. To her left she sees Alfie, the pub landlord, and Gemma, the hotel manager, rushing towards her.

"Out for a stroll Mrs. Dimbleby?" asks Alfie.

"Not right to stay indoors the whole day," says Gemma. "You know that as sure as I do, Mrs. Dimbleby. At school you always said 'Go out and breathe that fresh air'. Right as rain you was!"

Normally Diane loves having a good old chin wag with her fellow villagers—it's one of the many aspects of Apple Mews she adores. But today she wants to get on with her investigation, and without being watched. Doing so incognito might prove near impossible in her beloved village, at least at this time of day.

"We noticed the inspector detective go round yours around lunchtime…" says Alfie casually.

"It was about that dead man you found, weren't it?" asks Gemma, a little less casually.

Diane carefully considers what she should say to the questioning pair, all the while feeling like all the eyes of Apple Mews are watching her.

"Yes, Inspector Crothers did pay me a visit. He just needed to finish getting my witness statement, that's all."

Diane can see the two are not satisfied with this response. Their disappointment is not only due to being left out of hearing some juicy details—but their faces also reveal concern for the safety of their families and friends and of themselves.

"The inspector also told me there is nothing for Apple Mews to worry about," says Diane, knowing her words will be shared with the rest of the village within an hour or two. She hopes that this will alleviate any fear her neighbours might be feeling.

Nothing for Apple Mews to worry about... that's another way of saying that the case and its details are not the concern of anybody—except Inspector Crothers, his team and one shrewd mystery novelist—isn't it? Diane hoped her slight rephrasing of Darrell's direction brought the hotel manager, the pub landlord and the rest of the village some comfort.

"Maybe that means he just died of—what do they say on them copper shows—natural causes…" says Alfie

Diane does not acknowledge Alfie's optimistic statement. Instead she tells them she is looking for something "unrelated to the case" that she had dropped the day before, and that she is checking the village green to see if it had been dropped here. Now this is a blatant lie of course, but it might help disguise the fact that Diane is actually seeking clues to help solve the mystery of Paul Tucker's murder

Approaching the oak tree, Diane does not bother to put on booties or gloves. Although she would like to maintain investigative integrity, right now that would raise too many eyebrows.

Diane begins circling the old tree, and is startled to find, and nearly bumps into, Reverend Harvey, whose head is bowed in prayer. The vicar looks up and says, "Diane, you've arrived just in time."

"In time for what?" she asks.

"For a little impromptu service we're holding for the poor soul found here yesterday. We don't know who he is, or where he's come from, or whether he's a family man or single, or anything about him… we don't know how he died, whether he was brutally taken from this world, whether it was an accident, whether he was murdered… whether it was the result of a heated argument… whether he was caught in a love triangle… whether he's passed away from natural causes…"

Diane smiles politely, conscious of not divulging anything, not even the smallest of mannerisms.

"But," continues the Reverend, "we shall celebrate his life just the same and pray his soul is at peace now and forevermore."

The vicar nods his head, inviting the small group of villagers behind him to approach the oak tree. As Apple Mews' honorary barbershop quartet sings "Abide with Me" in four-part harmony, Diane slyly scans the grounds upon which they are huddled. She will want to mourn this stranger, oh yes, but after his murderers are stopped from doing this to anybody else and are locked away.

Once Reverend Harvey finally concludes his eulogy— an impressively long one considering he did not know the deceased—the small crowd departs, finally leaving

Diane alone to investigate. She stares across the green. For the first time since dawn, she is the only person she can tell is on the common, or anywhere in the vicinity for that matter. It strikes Diane as ominous as if suddenly she is the one who is ignorant of the facts, not the other villagers.

She quickly lets these anxious thoughts float away from her mind and starts examining the scene. This time, Diane starts at the very base of the tree and gets down on her hands and knees so that her eyes and nose are almost touching the ground. She feels the area where she had found the keycard—the burrow she had dug earlier. Her eyes and fingers seek out any items immediately adjacent to the hole.

Now up on her feet again, Diane slowly walks back and forth, following a strict grid system she has mentally drawn on the ground on all four sides of the tree. Something sparkles and Diane bends down. Picking it up, she determines it to be a silver sequin bead. If she were a woman who liked to gamble, she would bet the sequin had fallen off the bow tie of one of the barbershop singers.

At the same time as Diane picks up the sequin, a woman is finishing her afternoon run. She ends the workout with a final sprint through a section the green, then stops about 30 yards away from the scene Diane is investigating. She removes a water bottle from her waist pack and takes a long drink. Facing Diane's direction, she replaces the water bottle and stretches her calf muscles, one at a time, followed by each of her arms.

She slowly walks towards the closest bench without taking her eyes off the grey-haired woman who seems to be attentively staring at the ground while slowly pacing.

Suddenly an ominous feeling comes over Diane again. Her shoulders clench, her backbone shudders and she has that familiar, uncanny feeling she is being watched.

She turns around to see she *is* being watched. A young woman, maybe in her mid-to-late 20s, with long black hair, is staring right at her.

Calm down Diane, she thinks. It's obvious this woman has just gone for a run. Her face is flush, she's wearing a stylish pair of running tights with a matching T-shirt and she's stretching. Judging by her athletic and trim figure, running must be an important part of her regular routine. The young woman is probably just wondering what an older lady is doing alone, pacing, scrutinizing the lawn, analysing each blade of grass.

What a fool she must think I am!

Diane attempts to resume her land survey, but she feels conscious. She looks up again to see the young woman still fixated on her. Diane decides she had better leave this scene. The degree to which this woman is staring seems to go well beyond innocent curiosity. And Diane does not think she has ever seen this person ever before. Another stranger, the second one she's seen in 24 hours, in Apple Mews. This cannot be a coincidence. Non-locals only tended to visit Apple Mews during July and August or during the annual village festival.

Diane walks away from the oak tree towards the centre of the green, trying to present a leisurely pace. She is unsure of where she is retreating to. She passes the bench where the stranger is sitting, maintaining a large distance between the woman and herself.

Once several yards past, Diane looks back, only through the corner of her eye, to see the young woman stand. Diane quickens her pace, only slightly at first. She looks back, more obviously this time, to see the woman following her.

Diane begins to double her pace and stride and then breaks out into a jog. Sweat droplets begin to trickle into her eyes. Her breath quickens, not from physical exertion but from the panic that is starting to overcome her.

As Diane is about to reach the other end of the green, the black-haired woman steps right in front of her. She must have caught up and passed her by a few yards, and circled back to stop Diane from leaving the area.

Diane stops, nearly tumbling into the woman. She takes two deep breaths and asks, as calmly as she can muster, "Can I help you?"

"I am just curious," says the woman. "You looked like you were searching for something very important. Did you find what you were looking for?"

Chapter 5

Diane takes a step back. She eyes the woman she came close to knocking to the ground— or rather who came close to knocking her to the ground—for at least five long breaths.

When the woman had asked her 'Did you find what you were looking for,' Diane could have sworn there was a distinguishable timbre to her voice. She recognized an English accent certainly, but with some underlying characteristics—Eastern European perhaps?

"Important? I'm not sure what you mean," says Diane trying to sound as cheery as can be. "I dropped a receipt the other day. I thought I might have done so while walking home through the green. But it's not important—just an old lady fussing about keeping all her records in order."

The black-haired woman looks Diane straight in the eyes in a way suggesting that she does not believe her story. She smiles all the same.

"I'm Sergeant Benedek," she says, reaching out her hand. Diane takes the palm in hers to be met with a firm grip.

"Pleased to meet you," says Diane, not sure she really is 'pleased'.

"I'm working with Inspector Crothers on the case," says Sergeant Benedek, nodding her head in the direction of the oak tree, where she had just been watching Diane look for her 'missing receipt'. "He asked me to follow up with you… just a few questions. Would you mind if we grab a quick coffee?"

This is odd, thinks Diane. Why would Darrell send someone else to ask her questions? That wasn't his style. He liked to be out doing much of the investigative legwork himself. Plus, he rarely asked Diane *questions*. Their conversations were usually casual, at least on the surface, not a question-and-answer scenario. Deep down they were an exchange of ideas, a brainstorming session if you will, where each was goaded towards whodunit theories.

And who would go for a jog while they were on duty like this woman had just done? Unless running around a village is a technique this Sergeant Benedek uses whilst investigating the people who live close to a disposal site.

Still, Diane senses something is wrong with this picture. However, she makes sure to try and hide any sign of feeling distrustful.

"We can certainly have a coffee together," says Diane, "although I may have a cuppa. We can go to Helen's right over there."

As they walk towards Helen Bell's café on Apple Mews' main drag, Diane feels for her phone which is luckily inside her jumper pocket—lucky because she often forgets to bring the device with her, still favouring face-to-face conversations when she's out and about.

Although Diane rarely talks on her mobile, she frequently uses its recording function, which comes in handy during research sessions or when a story idea jumps into her head. For fear of her creative ideas flying away, she will often say them out loud and preserve them as an audio file.

Surreptitiously, Diane taps on the recording icon and presses the record button. She feels in her gut that any conversation with this so-called Sergeant Benedek must also be preserved. In short, Diane smells a rat.

Seeing Diane approach, Helen Bell throws down her piping bag, nearly knocking the cupcakes she's icing off the counter, and rushes to the door. She swings the door open and pulls Diane inside and into a hug.

"Well if it isn't Diane Dimbleby! It's been donkey's years since I've seen ye!"

True, Diane hasn't been to Helen's café in quite some time, never mind the fact they wave to each other at least twice a week while each is going here and there around the village.

"It's lovely to see you too Helen," says Diane, warmly, but not quite as warmly as her usual self.

Helen jabbers on about her grandchildren's loose teeth and how she finally took the plunge and ordered a cardie on *the Internet,* and how she is experimenting with brighter-coloured icings… all the while moving her head back and forth, looking pleasantly at Diane, and somewhat curiously, or skittishly, at the strange companion.

"Diane, you haven't introduced me to your… friend?" says Helen, her smile now fully disappeared.

"I'm Sergeant Benedek," says the young woman before Diane can answer. "And I'd like to order one coffee and one tea please."

Sergeant Benedek walks directly to the till to pay. It takes a moment for Helen to process what Benedek has demanded. Her easy-going café is not so customized to the sequence or style of this customer's requests. After a pause, Helen hurries behind the counter to accept the woman's note, taking a few moments to marvel at her straight and shiny black hair, before giving her the appropriate change.

Meanwhile, when the sergeant's back is turned, Diane quickly takes out her mobile and takes a picture of the young woman—she coughs to cover up the shutter sound effect. Diane sends the picture to Inspector Crothers. Walking as far away from the counter as she can in the cosy café, Diane dials his number.

"Darrell, hello," whispers Diane. "I sent you a picture... the woman in the picture, is she your sergeant?"

Before Diane can hear the inspector's answer, she feels a hand on her shoulder. Both her shoulders suddenly tense as she turns around.

"Shall we sit down?" says Sergeant Benedek with a chilly smile.

"Oh yes," laughs Diane nervously.

They sit at a round table covered with a purple lilac cloth. Helen hurries over with their hot drinks. Normally she would have pulled up a chair to join them, but she isn't exactly getting the warm and fuzzies from this Sergeant Benedek. She goes back to icing her cupcakes, but is quite capable of multitasking; her ears are ready to tune into her customers' conversation.

"Who were you talking to on the phone?" asks the sergeant, rather bluntly.

Most people with any common decency would not ask an acquaintance, let alone someone they just met, a question like that. Diane does not remember asking anybody that type of question, except maybe her late husband David. Now she might playfully ask Albert if somebody were to call him, but probably no one else.

The fact that this woman had the nerve to ask—even though the phone call did in fact concern her—confirms Diane's suspicions. This Benedek woman is no sergeant at all. Diane has the sinking feeling that she has fallen into a nasty trap. A passing thought enters her mind—*will I be able to escape?*

"Oh, that was just my son," says Diane, attempting nonchalance. "He wants to pop in tonight. He wanted to make sure I'd be home, that's all."

Benedek lets out a nasty titter. "Now Diane, I know you don't have a son."

Diane looks down, not quite sure of what to say or do next. It occurs to her that this is the first time this woman has called her by her name. It seems that Benedek knows for a certainty that Diane has no son or any children at all. What else does she know about her?

This could be worse than Diane's misgivings had originally imagined. She thought perhaps this imposter was a newspaper reporter pretending to be a police officer in order to get undisclosed information for her next story. Or perhaps even one of Paul Tucker's family members.

But this woman knew some of Diane's personal details. Diane could be caught in an even more sinister snare, and she isn't sure how to free her foot—or her neck—from its wire noose.

Diane looks up to see Benedek's eyes searching outside as if she is expecting someone or something. Otherwise, why would she and Diane be sitting here in Helen Bell's café, as if they were two friends catching up?

"Lovely day isn't it… those dark clouds I saw earlier, I was sure it was bound to rain, but it's not too bad today," Helen says after noting a lull in conversation—silence is uncustomary in her café.

Diane and Benedek nod their heads without saying a word. They each take a sip from their cups. Benedek takes her eyes away from the window and turns back to Diane.

"So you're the one that found the body," she says in a low voice so Helen cannot hear. She attempts a look of empathy, but Diane is not fooled.

"Yes, I found him, poor fellow," says Diane. "I thought he was just having a nap…"

Intentionally Diane does not reveal much more, especially nothing about the keycard she had discovered embedded in the ground next to the oak tree, nor the information Darrell had shared with her. She is determined not to tell Benedek, if that's her real name, that Paul Tucker's organs were ripped from his body and stolen away... although she is beginning to think that Benedek already knows this.

Diane finishes her cuppa and gets up to go to the bathroom. "Nature's calling," she says more light-heartedly. Although she does not trust Benedek, it's possible that Benedek thinks Diane is a naïve old woman—that Diane has believed her story about being a sergeant. Maybe she'll even decide to leave while Diane is in the bathroom, concluding that she knows nothing important about the murder.

Even now Diane is feeling quite jittery. She wonders if David had felt this way. She is still not exactly sure about the timing of his murder. Maybe he didn't even expect he was going to be killed. Did the robber sneak up on him, or did David see him coming? Did it happen quickly or did the robber make him suffer? If Diane were to truly take the time to think about it, it's probably all the questions that still surround her husband's death that drive her to answer questions about other vicious crimes.

Oh, I dearly hope he wasn't scared.

Inside the toilet stall she decides she better leave a message just in case. Luckily she still has her notebook and pen. She starts writing: *To anyone who reads this…*

When Diane exits the stall, Benedek is waiting next to the sink. Diane hadn't even heard her come inside the toilet room.

"Wash your hands and then we'll go," says Benedek calmly but confidently, revealing a knife in her hand.

It looks like a boning knife, Diane thinks, before the immediate threat to her safety sinks in. Whatever kind of knife it may be, the shimmer of the blade suggests it is sharp. Diane's mind drifts off to a scene where Benedek is engaging in a morning ritual of sharpening her knife collection as her coffee is brewing in the background. The daydream finally allows reality to set in. Diane's heart skips two, maybe three beats, before she washes her hands as was demanded.

"Move," Benedek whispers viciously as Diane dries her hands.

Benedek slips the knife handle up her sleeve and encloses the blade discreetly in her palm. She shoves Diane shoves towards the exit and follows close behind. Outside the toilet room, she orders Diane to walk to the café's exit.

Diane looks around for Helen but cannot see her. She must be in the back kitchen. Benedek shoves Diane reminding her to *Move!*

The café door opens and closes abruptly, sending Helen out to see who has newly arrived. But she finds the café empty. That's not like Diane to leave without saying goodbye, she thinks.

Helen scoots over to the window and sees Diane getting into the backseat of a stranger's car. Rather, the young woman who was accompanying Diane is pushing her into the car!

"That doesn't look right," says Helen out loud. "Not right at all."

The car screeches quickly away. Helen begins pacing back and forth wondering what to do. She doesn't like to meddle into people's affairs, but sometimes meddling is warranted, especially if a friend might be in trouble.

Helen suddenly remembers seeing Diane go to the toilet before she had gone into the kitchen to take the latest batch of cupcakes out of the oven. As if channelling some of Diane's gumshoe skills, Helen scurries to the lavatory. She checks each of the stalls for what… she's not quite sure.

"Diane, are you in trouble?" says Helen out loud, desperately pleading for an answer.

She mindlessly removes a piece of rubbish that is lodged between two of the stall doors. She throws it into the bin and heads back out to the café. *What to do? What to do?*

Subconsciously still feeling the texture of that piece of trash in her hand, she suddenly clues in that it had been a folded piece. She scurries back into the toilet room and removes the item from the bin. Helen quickly unfolds the piece of paper to find an enclosed message:

To anyone who reads this,

I might be in serious danger. There is a woman who is pretending to be a police sergeant working for Inspector Darrell Crothers. She calls herself Sergeant Benedek. Please call Inspector Crothers at the Shrewsbury Police Station and tell him.

Sincerely, Diane Dimbleby

"Thank you Diane!" whoops Helen, scurrying again out of the toilet room.

She runs behind the counter, nearly knocking the fresh tray of cupcakes to the ground, and searches through her purse for her mobile.

"Operator, get me the Shrewsbury Police Station... hello, is this the Shrewsbury Police? I need to talk to Inspector Darrell Crothers please. It's an emergency... hello Inspector Crothers? Oh thank goodness. Inspector, Diane Dimbleby is in trouble, grave trouble I fear! She was here in my café with a woman, a woman I don't know, and now I think she's been kidnapped. I saw that dreadful woman push her into a car, not the boot mind you, in the back seat, but she was being right forceful. No, drat, I didn't get the license plate... Helen how stupid can you be... yes, I'll wait here... come to Helen Bell's café, Apple Mews...I won't move a muscle... goodbye."

Helen is waiting outside in front of her café when Darrell arrives. She beelines it towards him before he's even exited his Range Rover.

"Try to stay calm," Darrell says kindly. "Let's speak inside."

Helen hurries the inspector inside her café and they sit in the same chairs where Diane and the suspicious woman had been sitting not long ago. Darrell asks Helen to tell him everything that went on, from the time Diane and the woman arrived at the café to the time she saw Diane being pushed inside the car.

"And what did the car look like?" asks Darrell.

"I can't be sure," says Helen, who hasn't driven a day in her life. "It looked big and I think it was dark blue or maybe black."

"That's alright. Now, what about the woman?"

"Oh, her I remember well. She was in her late 20s, a little taller than Diane I'd say. And very slender, not an ounce of fat on her. Oh and she had this long, black hair, right striking it was."

Darrell takes out his mobile phone and brings up the picture message that Diane had sent him not long ago.

"Is this her?" he asks, showing Helen the picture.

"Yes, I think so," says Helen. "Oh it must be, because look, she's standing in my café from the looks of the picture."

Where else had Darrell heard the 'long, black hair' description? He quickly remembers the manager at the Farmer's Refuge Inn talking about the 'real gorgeous bird' with 'beautiful long, black hair.' The manager, Silas Crocker, had said Paul Tucker was talking to her in the hotel lobby. Could this be the same woman?

"You did the right thing calling me, Ms. Bell," says Darrell. "And we're going to do everything we can to find Mrs. Dimbleby."

Darrell exits the café, his mind immediately working like billy-o to strategize how to find Diane, and before it's too late. She has no close family relations and does not live with anybody that the kidnappers could contact for a ransom request. Just in case, her cottage needs to be constantly monitored, he decides. Quickly walking to his vehicle, Darrell calls the station.

"Bob, I need you to put in a request to have a CCTV camera installed at Diane Dimbleby's home in Apple Mews immediately. We'll need someone watching the monitors round the clock. Better have plain clothes officers circulating around Apple Mews too and Mrs. Dimbleby's cottage too. We've got a possible kidnapping, so we're pulling out all the stops. Oh and Bob, see if you can track the location of Mrs. Dimbleby's cell phone. I think it's a smartphone so it should have a GPS locator on it. Cheers Bob."

At the station, Darrell is sitting with Silas Crocker, the manager of the Farmer's Refuge Inn. He's having Silas look at mugshots to see if he can recognize the woman with long, black hair among them. It's been a few hours since Darrell met with Helen Bell at her café and still there are no leads on where Diane has been taken.

"Look inspector, I pride myself on doing my bit for justice, but how much longer do I need to look through these mugs? The only reason I ask is because I have a date with this gorgeous bird. Beauty like that doesn't fall in my lap all the time if you know what I mean."

Before Darrell needs to coax Silas to keep looking at pictures of offenders, Sergeant Bob Webster comes rushing in.

"Sir, we found her phone," the sergeant says.

Darrell excuses himself from Silas so he can talk Sergeant Bob Webster in private.

"Where is she Bob?"

"About 20 miles outside Apple Mews… in a ditch, sir."

Darrell goes pale and nearly loses his footing. Diane in a ditch? That can't be good. Luckily the sergeant picks up on his inspector's worst fears.

"Oh sorry sir, only the mobile is in a ditch, not Mrs. Dimbleby. I had a nearby officer go to the spot to check. It looks as if the phone was thrown there."

Sergeant Webster leads Darrell to the board where the map of the area surrounding Apple Mews is pinned. He indicates the location where Diane's mobile was found. He points out that the road in question leads to a farm and not much else.

Darrell decides he cannot hesitate; he has to follow the lead.

"Good work Bob! I'm on my way to the farm. Do me a favour and radio for any officers in the area to—"

Before Darrell can finish saying his request, he feels his mobile phone vibrate. He takes it out of his pocket to see he's received a text message:

If you want to ensure Diane Dimbleby remains safe, keep reading. Diane's kidneys and liver will be removed tonight unless I receive £5 million. Money should be delivered to the Midlands Airport. Place the money & an airline ticket for Rio de Janeiro, Brazil inside a suitcase. The suitcase should be waiting for me at the airline counter. No police with the suitcase or the deal is off. Fr. 'Sergeant' Benedek.

Chapter 6

Lynn Benedek gets off the phone with one of her bosses. She called to let him know the ransom request was issued. The text message to Inspector Darrell Crothers is more or less reflective of what she had been instructed to send, the emphasis being on *more*. Her boss had directed her to request three *million pounds; she tacked on an extra two million plus a plane ticket to Brazil for herself.*

This is the first time in almost ten years that she's ever rebelled against her 'crime firm'. She's hoping it will be the last. Now 27 years old, Benedek had been recruited by The Dissociates, an organized crime element based out of Birmingham, when she was barely 18 years old.

With her above average intelligence and her determination, like that of a bulldog, she could have become anything she had set her mind to; she could have accomplished many noble acts and had many successes during her lifetime. Since she was a young teen, however, she had spent most of her time with the wrong crowd, using her intelligence for bad rather than good. Perhaps it was her rage at the world, which seemed to percolate consistently, just under the surface, and her desire to belong that led her to forge bonds with criminals.

Benedek had been adopted by a British couple when she was about three or four years old. Her new parents were wonderfully loving, but somehow their affection was never able to make the full journey to her heart. It was as if the perceived abandon by her natural parents traumatized the young girl forever.

Benedek's father had been a Soviet soldier stationed in Hungary, her mother a native to Budapest. When her father was forced to evacuate the country in the early 90s along with the rest of his fellow troops, Benedek's mother, heartbroken, felt she could no longer care for her young daughter.

In Benedek's world, being recruited by The Dissociates was a sure sign of success. And even though she had continued to move up the criminal ladder, she has come to the realization that she no longer can tolerate having anyone tell her what to do. But you could not ask to leave an organization like The Dissociates and expect to be able to carry on a normal, everyday life in England. Her only chance to start a new life was to flee the country, to go to Brazil.

In Brazil, Benedek could make a fresh start; perhaps lead a crime-free life. But she doesn't even have the desire to do that. She's most gratified, or at least thinks she's most gratified when she has loads of money—she believes that money can buy happiness. And the crime skills she's honed most of her life enable her to make a lot of money in a short amount of time, regardless of the people she hurts or maims—even kills—along the way. Benedek does draw one moral line, however; she is adamant against causing any harm to a child.

If she can just get through the rest of the day, outsmarting the police and her bosses, she'll make it to the other side of the world free from British law and her criminal umbilical cord.

Darrell is sweating bullets. He knows he should have listened to that little voice inside him saying, 'Don't involve a civilian in this investigation.'

But he did not listen. He let Diane get involved in the case of Paul Tucker's murder which possibly—no, probably—involved a highly organized crime ring of organ traffickers. Not only had Darrell let Diane get involved, but he had also encouraged her to do so. What was he thinking showing up at her cottage multiple times? The kidnapper or kidnappers could have been watching his every move.

If Diane is killed, it will be entirely my fault, Darrell thinks. His paranoia and panic set aside, Diane being 'eliminated' is not a far-fetched prediction. She's seen too much, knows too much, and would surely be able to recognize Benedek in the future.

"Bob, where are we with tracing that Benedek's mobile number?" yells Darrell, unable to completely hide his anxiety.

"I just spoke to Digital Forensics, Sir. It appears the suspect was using a burner phone so the number is not registered to anybody. Plus the phone's location cannot be tracked—the mobile must have been destroyed immediately after the text was sent."

"Crothers!" shouts the superintendent before Darrell can yell *Bloody hell!* "In my office...now!"

Darrell takes a deep breath and pauses for a moment to look at the picture of his family on his desk, before going in to see Superintendent Alan Moore.

Superintendent Moore could have retired last year, but probably will not do so for at least another five, nor should he. He is as fit to serve as head of the police station as he was when appointed to the rank ten years ago. He is scrupulous, and very much a no-nonsense kind of leader, but he is also fair.

"Crothers, please sit," the superintendent starts. "I understand you know this Diane Dimbleby from previous cases, and that you've involved her in this case beyond what is expected of a material witness. Have I gathered the right information or am I mistaken?"

"Yes sir, you are correct on all counts," says Darrell glumly. He understands that his actions could cost him a suspension, a demotion or even permanent dismissal. But this seems to pale in comparison to the possibility of Diane being killed. He would never forgive himself.

"Well, we will deal with that later," says the superintendent pragmatically. "First let's deal with finding Mrs. Dimbleby... and hopefully finding her alive."

Darrell is once again reminded why he respects his superior. He too will worry about how he himself will be reprimanded later and focus on the crucial task at hand.

"I've just been on the phone with the chaps down in the evidence room, and they've shared something quite fortuitous," the superintendent continues. "It turns out there is a substantial sum of forged notes down in the evidence locker. Remember that major counterfeiting case?"

Darrell remembers it well. It was a big win for the force. The money had fooled most counterfeit experts, which explained why the phony pounds had been very difficult to track or to catch the culprits. But the counterfeiters had been caught, convicted and have now behind bars for years.

"That's great news Sir," says Darrell, his mood suddenly changing to optimism. Normally he might worry whether it is too risky to use counterfeit funds, but not with these true-to-life notes. "How about the plane ticket to Brazil, Sir?"

"Yes, I'm authorizing the purchase of a one-way ticket to Rio de Janeiro. Now, what's your strategy to bring Mrs. Dimbleby home?" asks the superintendent, as much to boost the inspector's confidence as for protocol's sake.

It's done the trick. Darrell's fear is overtaken by his characteristic tenacity to close the case. He tells the superintendent that he is quite certain Diane was, and possibly still is, being held at the isolated farm down the road from where her mobile was discovered. The way he sees it, he can take two approaches.

One is to go immediately to the farm with armed police assistance and catch the kidnappers by surprise so he and his team can arrest them before they kill Diane. The alternative is for Darrell and several undercover officers to go to the airport, blend in with the crowd and then arrest Benedek (or whoever goes to pick up the ransom) before she can alert any of her accomplices.

Both plans are risky, and neither guarantee that the suspects will be apprehended and that Diane will be saved. But police operations are very much like life—

there are very few guarantees. Plus Darrell and his team can no longer hesitate.

After talking it out with the superintendent, Darrell realizes he does not need to choose, nor should he. He will execute both plans, and the superintendent agrees that this is the best strategy. Darrell thanks the superintendent and hurries out of his office. He needs to get the two teams ready for the farm and the airport operations as soon as possible.

"Attention everyone," he says, gaining the attention of the detective sergeants and constables around the room.

He gets the two teams organized arranging for armed assistance to accompany those headed to the farm and telling the airport group to prepare to change into plain clothes. Darrell will lead the farm team. He has his best man, Sergeant Bob Webster of course, lead the other group. He also tells Sergeant Webster to make sure they purchase the plane ticket, collect the ransom from the evidence room and place it in a suitcase before heading to Midlands Airport.

Once all the details are finalized, the superintendent imparts his full confidence to all of his officers, including Inspector Crothers. Darrell shares the sentiment with his constables and sergeants. Without wasting any precious time, the two teams depart.

While racing to the farm with lights and sirens on, Darrell hopes they have not forgotten any important details needed for the successful execution of these operations. It brings to mind the expression 'the devil is in the detail'—an expression Darrell often ponders. While he prides himself on often being able to catch a criminal through identifying their smallest of mistakes, he hopes this does not apply to his police force's current operations.

Darrell passes by the site where Diane's mobile phone had been found. He slows down to get an ample view of the ditch, just to make certain that Diane is, in fact, not lying there.

"Don't go barmy on me now Darrell," he has to tell himself momentarily before returning to original speed.

As they approach the farm, he gets on the radio telling his fellow officers to turn off their sirens and lights. "We don't want to give them any sign we're coming," he adds.

Darrell closes his Range Rover door as quietly as he can. He signals for the armed police team to surround the farmhouse and barn.

"All in place?" he whispers over the radio. "Remember, hold your fire unless absolutely necessary. And go!"

The armed officers burst into the farm buildings and move from room-to-room as they have been meticulously trained to do. Over the radio, Darrell can hear various voices yelling "Clear," denoting the absence of a threat in the series of sections they are traversing through.

When they determine that both buildings are completely deserted, Darrell immediately calls his sergeant. "Bob, at the farm here… no sign of Diane or Benedek or anybody else… you've just arrived at the airport? Got the suitcase in place? Good. Cheers Bob. I'll be heading there soon."

Before leaving the farm, Darrell asks his team to look for any signs that Diane and the kidnapper, or kidnappers, had been there. While searching the upstairs bathroom, Darrell himself finds something under the claw-foot tub. He picks it up. It looks almost exactly like a Shropshire Police badge—looks like, but Darrell can immediately tell it feels lighter. It must have been the badge Benedek was carrying whilst pretending to be a police sergeant.

Benedek pushes Diane out of the back seat of a car. Behind the driver's wheel is one of The Dissociates' soldiers.

"I'll wait for you in Section A of the parking lot," he tells Benedek.

She nods her head and the soldier drives away. What he doesn't know is that Benedek is not going to meet him afterward. She plans on leaving three of the five million pounds for her bosses in an airport locker—she will always feel at least some sense of loyalty, even gratitude towards The Dissociates—and when she arrives in Brazil, she'll send them an untraceable note letting them know the money is waiting for them. Any of the firm's soldiers have been trained to open such a locker in at least a dozen different ways.

"Move," hisses Benedek, discretely revealing to Diane that she is still carrying a sharp knife, as if Diane needs a reminder. "And if you show any sign of distress, say goodbye to your future as a best-selling author."

"I understand," says Diane calmly. Thank goodness for her yoga classes and her optimistic nature. After arriving at the farmhouse, Diane had made a conscious decision. It would do no good to panic or show any fear or anger. Her best chance of survival would be to be at peace with the situation, as much as one can be when they are kidnapped. Instead of wondering whether she will get out of this alive, she is watching Benedek's mannerisms and movements as if she is conducting character research for her next novel.

Humming show tunes under her breath has also been a godsend. As Benedek is 'escorting' her through the airport with the spine of the knife pressed into her back, Diane is softly humming "I'd Do Anything" from the musical *Oliver!*

Benedek walks them towards the airline counter where she sees the unclaimed suitcase waiting for her. She looks around to check if any security or police are in the vicinity. Secure in the fact that she does not see any uniforms, she picks up the suitcase.

Walking away, while nudging Diane along, Benedek says, "We're at an airport, and you're going to take a very long voyage, Diane."

Something in the way Benedek says those words sounds ominous to Diane. She knows she has to think fast or Benedek will get away and Diane... well, she could be gone forever.

"Bomb!!!!" screams Diane at the top of her voice, whilst simultaneously pushing Benedek away from her as hard as she can.

Diane's outcry is heard by practically everyone in the airport terminal. Within seconds, Sergeant Webster and two other undercover officers run towards the two women. Before they can even grab Benedek, armed police surround them and demand that they all drop to the ground.

When he arrives at the airport, Darrell sees a crowd of people surrounding what must be a spectacle of proportions. He moves through the crowd, showing his badge so he can get through. When he reaches the opening, he sees a circle of armed police officers pointing automatic weapons at five individuals lying flat on the ground. Even though their faces are pressed to the floor, he can pick out his sergeant Bob Webster, the long black hair presumably belonging to the woman who has been pretending to be Sergeant Benedek, and Diane.

"She's alive," Darrell whispers to himself with relief.

So as to not cause any of the armed airport police officers to react, Darrell slowly takes just a few steps closer. Sliding his badge across the floor towards one of the armed officers, Darrell explains to him that he's with the Shrewsbury Police, as are three of the gentlemen lying on the ground. He tells them they've been on a rescue mission and that both the victim and the kidnapper are lying on the ground.

Once the airport officer verifies Darrell's identification, he and his team allow the Shrewsbury officers to take Benedek into custody. Darrell helps Diane stands up and gently guides her away from the chaotic scene.

"Are you alright?" Darrell asks, fully revealing his concern.

Diane nods her head and closes her eyes.

"How can I help Diane? What can I do?"

"Take me home so I can have a cup of tea… or perhaps a whiskey!"

A few days later, Diane hears a knock at her cottage door. She opens the door to find a remorseful looking Inspector Darrell Crothers. He's a holding a clear bowl with a white water lily floating inside.

"You brought me a water lily?" says Diane beaming.

Darrell nods shyly. He's happy to see Diane smiling. He thought he might arrive to see her looking traumatized over the ordeal.

"And did you slap on your hip waders to pick this flower for me Darrell?"

Again the inspector nods.

"Well come through won't you, for a cuppa?"

Darrell enters, placing the vase delicately on top of the credenza before taking a seat on the sofa.

"Ta," he says, accepting the cup of tea from Diane. He stares at the cup's round-leaved sundew pattern again, with mixed feelings.

Diane sits across from him and smiles gently. She looks tired but placid.

"Diane, I am truly sorry for what happened to you," says Darrell. "I put your life at risk. I involved you too much in the case. I shouldn't have done that."

"Well Darrell, I think I pushed my way in, don't you think?" Diane laughs. "The way I see it, I knew the risks and I'm a big girl."

Darrell feels some of the weight lift off his shoulders. Knowing Diane is not cross with him allows him to take some satisfaction in his case soon coming to a close.

"I have to admit that even though we didn't follow protocol, without you I think we would still be searching for those dreadful organ snatchers," he says.

Darrell explains that because of her snooping, she found the first solid lead in the case—the keycard to the Farmer's Refuge Inn.

"And what about Benedek, if that's her real name…" asks Diane, shuddering, but just a little.

"Yes, her name is Lynn Benedek, and we've determined she's a member of an organized crime group out of Birmingham. They call themselves The Dissociates. We're starting to find out that stealing organs is just the beginning of their heinous crimes. It looks like Benedek's going to turn on her group and testify against her bosses."

Based on the time Diane had spent with Benedek, she still wasn't sure whether the woman was evil or simply lost. She'd like to believe the latter but will never know for certain. Whatever the case may be, it seems like this resolution—that the majority of the organized crime firm to which Benedek had belonged will be destroyed—will serve the greater good.

Epilogue

A pile of long black hair is accumulating around the bottom of a salon stool. A woman barely recognizes her reflection in the mirror; she doesn't remember ever seeing herself with short hair.

"You been living here long?" asks the hairdresser.

The woman shakes her head no.

When she was enrolled in the UK Protected Persons Service, in exchange for testifying against the captains and sergeants of The Dissociates, 'Lynn Benedek' became non-existent. Now she has a new identity and is living in a new place with a new name. It isn't the fresh start she had been hoping for—it isn't Brazil—but it is a clean slate.

It isn't like she left a family behind—she had already cut ties with her parents long ago. She is missing some of the people she had been 'working with', but she doubts that sense of loss will last long.

Now in a place, small or large as it seems depending on the day, where nobody knows her, the possibilities seem endless. Her history has not followed her. She can be whoever she wants to be. The Protected Persons Service even helped her get set up with a job. It does not challenge her much, but it pays for rent and food.

Whether she will stay there, find another job, or revert back to her crooked and high-paying ways remains to be seen.

Most of the time she feels safe, like nobody from 'before' can touch her. But sometimes she finds herself looking over her shoulder...

"Seems a shame cutting all this beautiful black hair," says the hairdresser. "Is this your natural colour?"

She nods her head yes, but asks the hairdresser to dye it red once she's done cutting.

Superintendent Moore suspended Darrell for two weeks. Darrell knows he could have been given a far harsher reprimand for implicating Diane too deeply into a criminal investigation. Plus, the suspension has turned out not to be a punishment at all. It has given Darrell the chance to do more of the things he enjoys and misses out on, like going to Chloe's football match and Jeremy's art show, having a lunch date with his wife or going fishing with his father's best mates.

Today Darrell is sitting on the edge of the brook, fishing rod in hand, next to 'Old Tom Walker' and 'Uncle Kenny'.

"You should get suspended more often, lad," says Tom.

"Are you trying to say you've missed me?" laughs Darrell.

"That, and you always remember to bring the beer," winks Kenny.

At tonight's session of 'mead and mystery,' Diane and Albert are enjoying some chocolate brownies—they had each baked a pan—along with a few fingers of cognac.

Albert sets down Diane's latest chapters and smiles approvingly.

"Your writing is as enticing as always," he says. "I especially love the bit where you describe the lad falsely accused of vandalizing that Abbey in, what is the name of the town again? Shrewsbury—excuse me, I meant to say, Harridan…"

"Are you suggesting my fiction is veering too close to reality?" Diane giggles.

"I'm suggesting, my dear, that your reality is not only stranger, but also more electrifying than fiction! And I think we both know what the theme of your next book will be…"

The End of Murder on the Village Green

Murder in the Neighbourhood

Chapter 1

Anyone looking for day-to-day tranquility would be more than happy to settle in Apple Mews. It is probably one of the most composed and calm villages in the county of Shropshire – at least from a bird's eye view and at street level.

By walking down Apple Mews' main lanes you would see what you would expect in most English villages: a hotel and a pub, a church and a café, a primary school and a community hall that hosts Saturday night dances, craft fairs, suppers and even festivities for some of the long-time villagers' milestone birthdays and anniversaries. Apple Mews also has a wee police station – it is only manned by one constable at a time. There is no need for a police force any larger, as the criminal element *rarely* punctures the homes, businesses, gardens and fields of Apple Mews.

Place a harpist in the middle of the village green or a Japanese water fountain next to the pub and villagers might shake their heads at first, but they too would accept their presence as compatible with the ambience of their community.

Diane Dimbleby is one of Apple Mews' most prominent – and loved – citizens. Most of the villagers younger than she were taught by Diane at some point in their lives. Although she never let her students dilly dally, she encouraged them to reach their full potential, and for that she was a favourite teacher to most. Diane spent most of her working years teaching in Apple Mews, and most of all her years living in Apple Mews.

For two years, Diane had lived in London with her late husband, David. They had fallen in love almost instantly when David was holidaying in Apple Mews. When they were married, Diane moved to London with him, since David was already serving as a police detective at Scotland Yard.

Although the pace of the big city was not exactly Diane's cup of tea, she relished learning as much as she could about her husband's line of work. It quite simply fascinated her. While David was not technically permitted to divulge any information about the cases he was working on, he could not refuse his wife's blue eyes and enthusiastic spirit.

Their marriage was an extremely happy one but cut much too short. When David was killed during the course of a robbery, it was an easy decision for Diane to move back to her home village and resume the profession she loved.

This time though, she had an additional pastime: crime solving, which she happens to be very good at, much to the dismay of Inspector Crothers of the

Shrewsbury Police, the closest major police station in the region. And now that Diane is retired, she spends much of her free time writing detective mystery stories, partly inspired by her own, real-life experiences.

This very Saturday afternoon, in fact, Diane is sitting at her computer, typing away. At this very moment, she is trying to contrive the perfect red herring for her latest crime novel. *I could trick the readers into thinking that the husband did it… no… too cliché.*

"*AAAAAAAaaaaaaaaaaaaa!*"

Diane is jolted back into reality by the sound of a terrifying scream. It sounded like a woman's scream. Diane feels spooked up and down her spine.

"*Ruff au au Ruff au au!*"

Now, that sound Diane recognizes immediately – it is Carys Jones' dog, Rufus, who clearly sounds distressed. His yap morphs into a howl. The mournful sound immediately propels Diane to her front door. Something must be dreadfully wrong. Carys has either had a nasty accident or… worse…. Diane does not want to think about that.

Without giving a second thought to red herrings, whodunits, or the slow-cooking crockery pot she just turned on a half-hour ago, Diane rushes out the door. Still in her slippers she runs – she is in marvellous shape for her 60-some years – to her friend Carys' house three doors down.

Unlike Diane, Carys Jones has not lived in Apple Mews her whole life. The long-time resident was immediately drawn to the new neighbour, and in recent years, the two ladies have shared numerous meals together and often enjoy chats over a cuppa.

Diane admires Carys' loving and caring nature and how she often volunteers for a homeless charity in Shrewsbury. Diane likes to bake cookies or make sandwiches to send along with Carys, but she admires how Carys regularly spends that face-to-face time with some of the area's most vulnerable individuals.

Arriving at her home, Diane sees Carys' front door wide open. Richard, one of Carys' caregivers, is standing in the front foyer, looking rather pale.

"Richard, what's happened?" shouts Diane, racing towards the entryway.

"I've called the ambulance and the police," says Richard shakily, pacing back and forth.

"The police!?! Ambulance! Oh dear, where is she?" Diane pushes past Richard towards the sound of Rufus yapping.

Inside the living room, Diane finds Carys awkwardly lying on the floor, her limbs splayed in every direction.

Rufus is next to his owner sensing that something is wrong. For a moment, Diane stares in shock at her friend who is eerily lying in complete stillness. Diane hurries to her side and kneels on the floor.

Careful not to shake her for fear of causing any more physical injury, Diane places a hand on Carys' back. She does not detect any movement.

"Carys," Diane whispers. "CARYS," she says louder this time, barely keeping a sob from escaping.

"I think she fell from the balcony," Richard says nervously. He kneels down next to Diane and points up above their heads.

Diane looks up to see the balcony's sturdy railing connected to a series of ornate spindles standing firmly in place. None of the parts appear to be cracked or missing.

"Did you see her fall?" asks Diane.

"No, I was in the kitchen preparing lamb casserole for Mrs. Jones' dinner. I heard her scream and…"

Diane nods her head. She stands up and walks back out into the hallway. Sifting through the shock, Diane feels in the pit of her stomach that Carys' death is more complicated than meets the eye. Perhaps it's best that Inspector Darrell Crothers gets involved. Although he might not realize that she thinks so, Diane regards him as the most dedicated detective she's ever encountered in the county of Shropshire.

She takes her mobile out of her pocket and dials the inspector's number. While listening to the ring-back tone, Diane gazes at Carys' photographs on the wall. One is of stalwart-standing Celtic crosses juxtaposing some crumbling stone ruins. Another is of a hilly pasture, lush with grass and sheep, overlooking the blue sea. Diane cannot remember where Carys had said these stunning pictures were taken...

"Inspector Darrell Crothers," says the 30-something Shrewsbury detective on the other end of the line.

"Oh Darrell... it's Carys... Carys Jones... she's... Apple Mews..."

"Diane, I've already been notified and I'm on my way," he says. "Now listen to me carefully. I don't want you anywhere near Carys' house. It is the forensic team's job, not yours, to process the scene. I'll be in Apple Mews soon."

Hanging up, Darrell hopes he wasn't too harsh with Diane, a woman he's come to regard almost as a second mum. Of course, a civilian, no matter how great a talent they have for sleuthing, should never get involved with a police inquiry. And sometimes Diane did not always think the rule applied to herself.

Diane and Darrell have worked on a couple of cases together already - not that he would ever admit this openly for fear of getting into more trouble, or perhaps to preserve his pride. But the truth is, through their unconventional crime-solving collaborations, a sense of mutual respect has ripened between the two. Their relationship has survived a few trying times of late, not the least of these a kidnapping by a dangerous member of a crime firm that specialized in illegal organ trafficking.

Diane is not happy that Darrell asked her to stay away from Carys' house, but she cannot fault the inspector for following protocol. Her gumshoeing has already gotten him into trouble at least once, plus she would not later want to be accused of messing up a crime scene.

I'll just take one quick look around and then I'll leave, Diane thinks as she noses around the ground floor. In the kitchen, she admires the vase filled with sunflowers sitting on the counter. She realizes that other than the floral décor, the counters are empty.

Diane hurries back into the living room. Richard is sitting on the couch holding his head in his hands.

"I thought you said you were preparing Carys' dinner…" Diane says carefully.

"I… I… I was just about to start…"

Diane stares at Richard for several moments until her eyes travel back to Carys lying on the floor. This time, she really lets herself look at her friend: her tightly closed eyes, her contorted mouth... *Did Carys feel excruciating fear during her last moments of life?*

Diane runs out of the living room and out of the house to find some shelter in the corner of Carys' garden. There she crouches down, bends her head to her knees and allows herself to wail for the first time. Her huddled position muffles the sounds of her deep sobs emerging from the bottom of her abdomen.

She is not startled by the hand now resting on her shoulder. She stands to see, expectantly, her 'partner against crime'.

"Oh Darrell," Diane cries. "Carys is dead, she's really dead. You know... she said, just the other day, that her greatest fear was dying alone. But this is much worse! Who would do this?!? Carys wouldn't hurt a fly!"

Diane continues crying almost uncontrollably. Darrell has never seen her like this before. He puts his arm around her and pats her back until Diane's sobs dwindle into sniffles. The awkward motions of the inspector, who is trying his best to comfort her, make Diane giggle just a little. She's starting to regain some composure.

"Now Diane, do not jump to any conclusions," Darrell says finally. "It has not yet been determined whether she lost her balance or got distracted and fell, or whether she was, in fact, pushed to her death."

"Well, one thing is certain. Carys did not jump from that balcony," says Diane adamantly.

"So you're saying she would *not* have committed suicide?" asks Darrell.

That is exactly what Diane means. She explains that Carys had no reason to do so. Just the other day she was sharing how fulfilled she felt and how blessed she was to have no stresses in her life. Sure, she wasn't as spry as she used to be, but she still managed to do many things on her own even help the homeless folks in Shrewsbury. Her caregivers just helped her out with certain tasks later in the day and with the 'heavy lifting.'

Besides, this would be the least plausible time Carys would take her own life. It had always been her dream to take a Mediterranean cruise, and this winter she was finally going to do it. The entire trip was already booked. Diane remembers chuckling at her friend the day she went through her thick stack of brochures advertising all of the different packages to choose from. *Now this one has more stops in Greece... but this one goes all the way to Istanbul... oh, but this one has tango and cha-cha-cha dance classes right on the ship!*

Diane laughs to herself, remembering her friend's almost frenzied planning. It was so good to see Carys so excited. She deserved to be happy. Tears begin to well in Diane's eyes again.

"This may have all been just a tragic accident," says Darrell.

"Something tells me that it was no accident, Darrell," says Diane. "Carys Jones was carefulness personified."

According to Diane, Carys was prudent in everything she did. For instance, she could walk just fine without a cane, but whenever it was slippery or wet outside, Carys would take her cane with her, even just to walk to a neighbour's or to the grocers down the road. There were so many new things she wanted to try and activities she wanted to keep on doing. She didn't want a broken leg or fractured arm to get in the way, especially not in the way of her commitments to help others.

"So you think someone pushed her?" asks Darrell.

"Except I have no idea who would want to kill Carys! I can't think of anybody with a motive to do so. Everybody adored her."

Their conversation is interrupted by the sound of a dog squealing, heard even above the sound of all the first responders on the scene and the onlookers starting to convene across the street. Diane and Darrell look over to see Rufus, Carys' dog, squirming in Richard's arms. He sees Diane and the inspector staring at him, sets the dog down and approaches them slowly.

"I was just trying to comfort poor Rufus," says Richard meekly.

"I'm Inspector Darrell Crothers. May I ask who you are?"

"He's—" Diane starts to be say, but is stopped by a stern glance from the inspector.

"Richard, Richard Butler. I'm one of Mrs. Jones' caregivers."

"And you are the one that discovered the body… er… discovered Mrs. Jones?"

Richard nods his head forlornly.

"When did you find her?" asks Darrell.

"I arrived for my shift at four o'clock this afternoon…" says Richard.

"You found Mrs. Jones when you arrived here then?"

"Yes."

"But Richard, you told me you were in the kitchen when Carys fell!" Diane pipes in.

"Is that true, Richard?" Darrell inquires.

"Yes… yes… sorry, I'm just a little agitated. She was my employer for the last two years after all," says Richard, wiping sweat from his forehead with his handkerchief.

"Just take a breath Richard, and when you're ready, tell me the series of events from the time you arrived here."

Richard heeds the inspector's advice and continues: "I arrived here a few minutes before four o'clock. I like to come a few minutes early to have a chat with Mrs. Jones before commencing my work. So I did that today, like any other day. We talked about her cruise – she is so enthused… she *was* so enthused about it – and we talked about what I should cook for dinner. She decided on lamb casserole. As I went into the kitchen, she said she was going upstairs to take a short nap. Not long after, Mrs. Jones fell."

"And what happened in between you arriving in the kitchen and Mrs. Jones falling?" asks Darrell.

Richard hesitated for at least half a minute before answering, "I started making the casserole of course."

"But you didn't, Richard," says Diane, trying to minimize any sign that she suspected he was lying. "The kitchen was immaculate when I went in there."

Darrell again darts his eyes disapprovingly at Diane. Whether he is disappointed that she has interrupted his line of questioning or that she walked around Carys' home, Diane is not sure.

"One last question, Richard," says the inspector. "You mentioned you are just one of the caregivers Mrs. Jones employed?"

"Yes, myself and Brian serve... served... as Mrs. Jones' caregivers. Brian started working here perhaps six months ago. At the moment he's away on holiday with his mother. Mrs. Jones is still quite independent, so she did not mind him taking some time away. She's so kind to everyone she meets..."

"And I'm assuming you and he both have a key to the house?"

Richard nods his head, yes.

"Thank you for your time, Richard," says the inspector. "I think you should go home and try to relax. Situations like this are quite traumatic for anybody who encounters them."

Before Richard takes his leave, Diane nudges the inspector and whispers under her breath for him to take down the man's contact information. Darrell bites his tongue to keep himself from losing his temper, but agrees with Diane's recommendation and asks Richard for his phone number and address.

When Richard leaves, Diane walks away from the traffic of all the police personnel and the curious bystanders. She finds a bench in a secluded section of Carys' garden – the same bench where she and Carys had spent several sunny afternoons chatting away.

Diane concludes that Richard Butler is hiding something. Exactly what though, she is not sure. She did not like to 'jump to conclusions', as Inspector Darrell Crothers had nearly accused her of. She liked to keep a clear head and focus on the facts like any respectable investigator would.

But Richard's inconsistent stories of what happened are certainly worth looking into, aren't they? First, he said he was cooking when Carys fell. Then he retracted that and said he had not quite started cooking. Then he told Darrell that he found Carys when he arrived for his shift at four o'clock. Then he reverted back to the cooking story.

Diane tries to recall her impressions of Richard from before today. She had not really given him much thought until now, even though she had met him numerous times. He always seemed very polite and willing to do anything to help Carys.

But what did Diane *really* know about him? With her, at least, Richard rarely if ever shared anything about himself.

Had he shared any personal information with Carys?

Chapter 2

A dozen or so villagers – most of Apple Mews' main street residents, plus whoever they had a chance to ring – are standing behind the yellow police tape surrounding Carys Jones' property. The men and women barely speak above a whisper; otherwise they hold their gazes towards the ground, all the while taking quick peeks to see if they can spot anything that can shed some light on what's happened inside Carys' home.

The crowd's sombre mood is suddenly lightened, albeit temporarily. The cause of their mild laughter – anything more would just be disrespectful – is a man who has just arrived on the scene. He is wearing a dark cloak and a dark Derby hat, and sports an unkempt, long white beard, quite obviously a fake.

The laughter soon dissipates, the crowd quickly remembering their solemn roles, as the man approaches Inspector Crothers.

"Hello Darrell," says Dr. William Jackson.

"William, you're looking right posh," chuckles Darrell. "And my oh my, you sure can grow a beard quickly. Why just the other day you were freshly shaven."

"Ha ha! It was my turn to lead the Charles Darwin tour in Shrewsbury" explains the medical examiner. "I got the call to come here just as we were leaving The Dingle. I don't suppose the tour participants will still be waiting for me after this…."

Darrell takes Dr. Jackson inside to show him where Carys Jones is lying on her living room floor. "Oh dear, this does not appear to be a peaceful passing," the medical examiner says.

Taking off the Derby hat and costume beard, he passes them to the inspector. He puts on a pair of gloves and surveys the entire body before him.

Walking around to Carys' head, Dr. Jackson squats down and gently moves her eyelids. Cupping her jaw with both hands, he tests to see if he can lower it. Lightly he bends her neck up and down.

"Rigor mortis has not yet set in," the doctor states.

Darrell looks at his watch – 5:30pm. "That basically confirms the timing our witnesses reported that the… incident happened."

"*Basically?*" questions the medical examiner.

"Yes, basically," replies Darrell. "One of our witnesses seems to be a bit confused about when he got here and whether Mrs. Jones was still alive when he did. He may just be a tad emotional though."

Dr. Jackson eyes the inspector, giving a glance denoting that any doubt Darrell might have is certainly worth investigating further.

The doctor then turns to his notebook and begins writing details about the exact positioning of Carys' body. Although a forensic photographer is taking crime scene photos, Dr. Jackson likes to rely additionally on his first-hand observations that are not apparent in even the highest resolution photographs. *Although a fall from a significant height, i.e. balcony, seems apparent, the cause of fall cannot be determined at this time*, he writes.

Once done performing his exam at the crime scene, Dr. Jackson asks if someone local can provide a formal identification of the body, or whether they should wait until she is brought to the morgue. Darrell suddenly remembers that the victim is a close friend of Diane's.

The inspector finds Diane outside, still sitting on the bench in a secluded section of Carys' garden, appearing lost in thought.

"Diane," he calls softly.

Who is he really, she wonders.

"Diane," Darrell calls again.

Her ruminations of Richard quickly stop once she hears her name; she blinks to realize she is still sitting in her dear friend's yard. Rufus, her dear friend's dog, is seeking solace at her feet.

"Hi there dear Rufus," she says, petting the fur on his neck.

"Diane, I'm sorry to bother you. We need somebody to identify the body… formally… with the medical examiner here. All we've been able to determine so far is that her relations are in Wales. Would you mind?"

Diane shakes her head at first. The thought of going back into that house where her friend is lying dead sends chills down all her bones. But gradually her head-shaking transforms into a tentative nod, and she agrees.

She slowly follows Darrell back inside. She sees Dr. Jackson next to Carys. He's writing, almost feverishly, inside a notebook. For a moment her mind lapses, and she's convinced he's a newspaper reporter coldly lapping up the gory details of a woman's mortality.

He's the medical examiner, Diane reminds herself, taking slow, almost childlike steps towards him and her friend.

"William, this is Mrs. Diane Dimbleby. She lives a few houses down," says Darrell.

"Mrs. Dimbleby, thank you most kindly for your assistance. Do you know this woman?"

Diane bursts out into renewed sobs and hides her head in Darrell's chest. "It's my friend, my dear, dear friend, Carys Jones," she manages to say in muffled gasps.

"She confirms it's Carys Jones," Darrell interprets. He holds Diane and for a moment has to keep her from falling to the ground next to where her friend is lying. Then, he slowly walks Diane back outside.

Darrell's sergeant, Bob Webster is waiting in the garden holding a leash attached to Rufus, Carys' little dog.

"Sir… Mrs. Dimbleby. I was just looking for you. I thought I might ask a favour. It will take a day or so before we can take Rufus here to the RSPCA. I wondered if you'd mind looking after him in the meantime. I saw you sitting on the bench earlier – he sure seems to have taken a liking to you."

Diane smiles a little. "I'd be pleased to. Rufus and I are good friends." She kneels down and scratches behind Rufus' ears. "We've taken some nice walks together, haven't we," Diane says.

As her hands move down to pat Rufus' neck and back she notices an oval-shaped locket hanging on his collar. It's stainless steel and blends in almost perfectly with Rufus' grey fur. *Hmmmm, that's curious…*

Diane does not think anyone else has noticed. She does not want to attract anyone's attention to it, not yet anyway. She loves being the one to discover potential clues. She'll open the locket at home, and if it turns out to be anything, she'll positively let the inspector know.

"I can take Rufus for as long as you need," says Diane. "I'll be off now. Darrell, you know where to find me."

Diane leads Rufus through two hedges in order to avoid the crowd of villagers still looking for answers. In almost any other case, Diane would enjoy speaking to each of them, but not today.

When they reach the road, Rufus stops and stands firmly in place. He looks back at his home and whimpers.

"I know you're sad, boy," Diane whispers in his ear. "I am too."

Rufus lets himself be pulled away. Diane decides they both need to go for a long walk before going home. She decides they'll go visit Albert, but that they will take the wooded path through the green instead of the more direct route – less chance of running into anybody that way.

When their feet hit the path, Diane finally feels like she's able to catch her breath and surface, just a bit, from the shock. Rufus' pace starts to quicken; he's like his old self, happy to be outdoors. Diane removes his leash and he runs, barking after the sound of a woodpecker hammering away.

Diane rolls back her shoulders and bends over to stretch her back. Continuing to walk, she tries to be aware of the full sensation of her feet touching the cushioned path to get her mind off the trauma she and Rufus have both experienced.

Rufus runs back with a stick in his mouth. Diane giggles and obligingly throws the stick for him a little way down the path. Rufus bounces after his newfound toy and scoops it up in his mouth effortlessly. He brings it back, and Diane throws it a little farther.

She can hear footsteps on the gravel behind her. *Oh drat, is that somebody nosing about?* she thinks. It would be rude to ignore them though. She turns around, except there is no one behind her. *My mind must be playing tricks on me.*

Rufus returns with the stick, urging Diane to keep on playing. She does not oblige this time. "I want you to stay close Rufus… we're almost there."

She hears what sounds like footsteps again. They sound closer and faster than the last time. In her peripheral vision she sees a figure approaching.

Her body is no longer relaxed. Diane rapidly fastens Rufus to his leash and begins to run. Rufus willingly follows and overtakes her, propelling Diane to run faster. She hears the follower's footsteps quicken behind them.

Diane looks straight ahead to see the end of the path and a stretch of houses about 100 yards away. Her feet suddenly get caught up in a massive tree root that crosses the path, and she falls to the ground, badly bruising her knees. Hearing the footsteps drawing near, she struggles to stand herself up and begins sprinting with the help of her canine companion.

At the end of the path, Diane can see Albert's house. "We're almost there," Diane encourages herself more than Rufus, as they continue their quick pace to her friend's front door.

Diane knocks unrelentingly until Albert swings the door open. She practically pushes him inside so that she and Rufus can enter hastily, then slams the door shut.

"Did you see him?" Diane screams.

"Who?" shouts Albert, alarmed and concerned for his friend.

"Richard!?! I think he was following us!"

"I didn't see anybody Diane. Here, come sit. You too Rufus. I'll get you a cup of tea."

Albert gently ushers Diane to one of his comfortable armchairs and goes out to the kitchen. Diane leans her head into the back of the chair and closes her eyes. Rufus jumps into her lap.

Albert soon comes out with a hot cup of tea – just how Diane likes it – and a bowl of water for Rufus, then sits in a matching armchair across from Diane.

"Now, have you caught your breath?" he asks.

Diane nods her head and takes a long sip of her warm drink.

"Who is Richard? And what's got you in such a state?"

"Richard is Carys' caregiver!"

"Oh, that's right... how is Carys anyway?"

"Albert! You haven't heard?!?!"

"Heard what?"

Albert had spent the whole afternoon indoors sifting through online newspaper archives. He is a major history buff, and one of his personal projects is cataloguing the county's most important headlines from the late 1700s until the present day. It is a time-consuming project that requires some degree of perseverance, but as Albert likes to say with a chuckle, "It keeps me out of trouble."

This afternoon had been particularly interesting - he had been reading all about the master engineer Thomas Telford – and so he had been far too distracted to know about Apple Mews' goings-on today.

"Albert…Carys is dead!"

"Oh dear! I wasn't expecting that."

Diane describes the ordeal of seeing her friend lying on the living room floor, looking so broken, so still. She feels comfort after sharing this with Albert. She is so lucky for his friendship and companionship.

Although Albert has not been as close to Carys as Diane, he has enjoyed their conversations. Plus, he knows how upsetting this is to Diane.

"So why were you running away from Richard?" Albert asks.

"I don't know if that was him. Maybe it wasn't anybody. Maybe I'm going mad."

"But why are you scared of Richard? He seems like a stand-up chap."

"He's hiding something Albert. He's the one who found Carys."

"Do you think he did it? I thought it must have been an accident… oh dear!"

"I don't know Albert…."

Diane decides she best be heading home. Her stomach is starting to growl – her dinner has probably cooked more than enough inside the crockery pot – and she should feed Rufus too. Diane asks Albert if he would like to come over for some stewed vegetables and chicken.

"I should have known that is on the menu tonight," Albert kids. He knows her tastes all too well. Diane's not a vegetarian, but vegetables are her favourite foods to eat, plus they are cheaper than most other ingredients. She'll complement veggies with fish or poultry – rarely, if ever, with pork or beef – and sometimes she's happy to eat vegetables alone.

Albert declines the dinner invitation as he himself is cooking a roast so that he can have for dinner and sandwiches for lunchtime tomorrow. He says he'll walk Diane home though.

Normally Diane would laugh off such an offer, but today she's glad he asked. When they are outside her house, both Diane and Albert first walk up to Carys'. The crowd is gone, the front door is shut and not an emergency vehicle is in sight.

"The forensic team must have completed their examination," says Diane, pulling Rufus away and back towards her home.

She hugs and thanks Albert and goes inside, detaching Rufus from his leash. He's been inside her home a handful of times but sniffs around as if it is the first time. His nose leads him to the kitchen and the attractive aroma coming from the crockery pot.

"Let's have some dinner, shall we Rufus?"

Diane suddenly remembers she forgot to grab Rufus' food bag and bowl from Carys' house. She'll have to wait until Monday when she can get a hold of the landlord for the house key.

"In the meantime, it's people food for you," says Diane.

She serves herself a plate of vegetables and chicken and fills a small bowl for Rufus. She sets the bowl down on the floor, and Rufus practically inhales the contents with delight.

"I should take that as a compliment, I gather?" Diane asks.

She decides she needs something a little stiffer than a cup of tea with her dinner, so stands on her tippy toes to reach in the cupboard for that bottle of red wine she's had for months. She suddenly remembers that Carys had given her the pinot noir for her birthday.

Diane digs out the wine opener, pulls out the cork and pours herself a generous glass. *To you, Carys.*

She takes her dinner and glass out to the living room with Rufus following close behind. She sits on the couch and turns on the television. The news is on. Diane starts eating her supper while giving Rufus nibbles of her chicken. She suddenly tunes into what the newscaster is saying:

"A 63-YEAR-OLD SHROPSHIRE WOMAN DIED THIS AFTERNOON FROM AN APPARENT FALL INSIDE HER APPLE MEWS HOME. THE POLICE HAVE NOT CONFIRMED WHETHER THE FALL WAS AN ACCIDENT OR OF A SUSPICIOUS NATURE. HER NAME WILL NOT BE RELEASED TO THE PUBLIC UNTIL ANY AND ALL FAMILY RELATIONS HAVE BEEN NOTIFIED…"

"You're certainly her family, Rufus," Diane says, ruffling the fur around his neck.

Diane can't remember Carys talking much about any relatives. *Had she mentioned anybody before?* While Diane pats Rufus her hand rubs up against his collar. *The locket!*

"I nearly forgot, Rufus," she says, holding the locket in her hand. She carefully removes it from the collar and tries to open it. Her fingernails are too short to slide inside the catch. She runs into the bathroom to fetch her nail file and goes back to the couch where Rufus is still sitting. She slides the nail file inside the catch and opens the pendant. A mini scroll of paper and a key fall out.

She picks them up off the floor and examines them. *This might be a mailbox key*, she thinks. She unrolls the tightly-wound piece of paper. It reads:

"4u opn sdb 2914 at bk."

Diane immediately understands what it means: "For you to open the safety deposit box 2914 at the bank."

Surely Carys wrote this note and hid something very important in her safety deposit box at her bank. This must mean she knew she was in danger. But for how long did she know? *I so wish she had told me.* The thought of Carys living in fear for any amount of time makes Diane's heart drop.

"You were such a brave guardian of this important message," says Diane, giving Rufus a little hug.

What on Earth could be hidden away in her safety deposit box, wonders Diane. Carys was not always bountiful with sharing personal information, but Diane never once thought she might be hiding any dangerous secrets. She seemed to live such a serene life. If Carys, whom Diane considered a good friend, had another life that Diane knew nothing about, it just goes to show that you can never really know a person fully. Diane likes to think she knew David almost completely… and now perhaps Albert.

Inspector Darrell Crothers should know about the safety deposit box. Diane looks at her watch – 10 o'clock. Perhaps it's too late to telephone him. Besides, it's a Saturday night, and the bank will not be open until Monday, she thinks.

This demonstrates the state of shock that Diane still finds herself in. Normally she would know, as any seasoned detective would (professional or otherwise), that an investigation does not stop on the weekend. An inquiry, particularly of a *suspicious death*, can occur 24 hours a day, any day of the week. She could call the inspector who would then call and make sure a bank manager is there as soon as possible.

But on this particular Saturday night, Diane is not thinking very clearly. Normally death or even the sight of a body does not shake her, nor dull her senses or make her numb. She has a stomach for this kind of thing… normally. Unless the corpse belongs to someone she knows and cares about deeply.

Luckily this has not happened very frequently in Diane's 62 years. The only other time her body and mind were so tense, so alarmed, so fazed, was when her David had been killed. It was surely a godsend that it was not she who discovered the body. Still, it was an event in Diane's life she wishes she could forget, but never will.

Diane returns to watching television, making a mental note to call Darrell in the morning. Flipping through the channels, she does not even bother to pay attention to what's up on the screen. Her mind is too busy thinking about what might be tucked away inside Carys' safety deposit box.

Her cell phone rings, and out of habit rather than wondering who's ringing at this hour, Diane picks it up to answer.

"Hello," she says distractedly.

"Hello Diane, it's Darrell."

She pauses for a moment and her eyes widen. "Oh, did I call you after all?"

"No, I called you," the inspector laughs.

"Oh yes," Diane says, still a tad confused. "I was thinking of calling you. But then I thought it was too late for you. It's not too late for me. I'm still slowly getting through my dinner. I just thought you might be reading to your little ones right now and tucking them in. Or surely they're already in bed..."

"Yes, they're sound asleep," Darrell replies. "Diane, I wanted to check and see how you were coping..."

"Forget about that. Have I got some news for you!" she says.

Chapter 3

Darrell knows that when Diane Dimbleby has news, she's not talking about a prize-winning jam or Princess Charlotte's latest outfit. It means she has *important* news; moreover, it's probably news that concerns the case of Carys Jones.

"Oh?" Darrell says inquiringly to Diane over the phone.

"I found *something*! Why don't you come round for a glass of wine and I can tell you all about it," Diane says. "That is, unless you're still on duty."

Darrell looks at his wife, Claire, who is lying beside him in bed. She looks up from her book, knowing that this particular pause in Darrell's voice and the look he's giving her this very moment means he wants to go "back to work." Claire knows better than anyone that when he's working a case, he's like a dog with a bone. And when a piece of evidence potentially presents itself after the sun goes down or in the middle of the night, Darrell is not one to wait until a more reasonable hour to investigate.

Claire nods her head for him to go ahead and gleefully mouths the words, "But you're doing the wash for the whole week."

Darrell chuckles. *I've got the best wife in the world,* he thinks.

"What's so funny Darrell?" Diane asks over the phone.

"Oh… nothing, nothing," he says, hugging the phone between his ear and his shoulder while hopping into a pair of slacks. "I'll head over right now."

Darrell kisses Claire's forehead, and she whispers "Be careful." He runs down the stairs and out the door. Unlocking the door to his Range Rover, Darrell is racking his brain trying to figure out what Diane has found. It surely has to do with Carys Jones.

Darrell is glad that Diane has come up with something and invited him over. Otherwise, it would have been a long night for him of tossing and turning and of his mind racing wondering who killed Carys Jones – he'd had a conversation with Dr. Jackson an hour ago confirming her death was no accident. Still the competitive nature he and Diane share – completely amicable of course – drives Darrell to think, *why does she always discover the good stuff?*

The inspector laughs the thought away and sets off for Apple Mews. He arrives no more than 15 minutes later – a little quick for Shropshire roads, but being the responsible law enforcement man he is, he had barely gone over the speed limit the whole drive.

Darrell runs up to Diane's front door and, forgetting to knock, bursts in. It seems that the excitement of finding out about Diane's "news" has made him forget his manners.

Diane looks up from the couch and howls with laughter at the detective's grand entrance. Darrell blushes and takes refuge in patting Rufus' head.

The thought suddenly hits him - this poor dog has lost his mother and still he's as sweet-natured as can be. Darrell does not know the dog well, but he wonders if he might still see a glimpse of pain in Rufus' eyes. He affectionately caresses the dog, who responds with a welcoming bark.

Darrell gets up and shyly takes a seat in the armchair facing Diane.

"Have you had supper already?" asks Diane.

Darrell hesitates. He had supper – Claire heated him up a piece of her delicious cottage pie – but the leftover aroma of Diane's crockery cooking awakens his sense of hunger.

"Of course you haven't," Diane winks. From the kitchen, she brings back a plate of vegetable and chicken stew and a glass of wine.

"Ta," Darrell says, and without hesitation, begins devouring the food before him. For a moment, he forgets his purpose for coming here in the first place.

"I have a question for you," Diane says. "Would a bank ever consider opening its doors on a Sunday… if you, let's say, needed to access a certain safety deposit box… as part of an investigation…?"

Darrell stops shovelling the food.

"Yes," he says after swallowing a mouthful. "A bank manager will even open a vault if necessary. But why do you ask?"

Diane taps her leg and whistles. Rufus runs up to her and jumps on her lap.

"He's really taken a liking to you already," Darrell admires.

"A vault would be perfect. Do you see this locket?" Diane says, pointing to the charm dangling on Rufus' collar. "Well, I found this message inside."

She passes him the small scrolled piece of paper. He opens it and reads: *4u opn sdb 2914 at bk.*

"Wow! Excellent find Diane! I'll have to get Liam from Forensics on this. He's a master at cracking codes. I wonder if it's a substitution cipher…"

"You don't have to ask Liam for help. You can solve it right now, Inspector. Pretend a teenager has just sent you a text message. Now read it."

"For you... open... sdb... what does *sdb* stand for?" Darrell says out loud. "……….. Oh! Safety deposit box – that's why you were asking about the bank! Of course. Well, I'm a bloody fool!"

Darrell shakes his head and smiles at his friend. He tells Diane that he will make arrangements with Carys Jones' bank in Shrewsbury.

"We should be able to go as early as tomorrow morning," he says.

"What do you mean, *we* can go tomorrow?" asks Diane. She remembers times in the past where she's perhaps stuck her nose in a little too close to the heart of an investigation.

"I don't think there's any harm in you coming to the bank with me on a Sunday morning when everyone is at church or still asleep in bed," he says. "Plus, it's only fair since you found the clue telling us to go to the bank."

"Maybe Rufus should come too then, since he guarded the clue so well," Diane giggles.

Her laughter soon turns to heartache, as her mind wanders to Carys who might have planted that clue in Rufus' locket out of fear for her own life.

Darrell takes the last bite of Diane's delicious stew and brings his plate to the sink. "You know, it appears that your instincts have been right… *again*," he calls out from the kitchen.

"Is that right?" says Diane, wiping away a few tears from her cheek.

"That Carys' death was no accident and that—" Darrell stops suddenly when he comes out to see Diane looking upset. "Maybe I should not talk about this… you're too close to the victim."

"No Inspector! Sorry… Darrell… it is because Carys is so important to me that I want to know every detail possible."

Darrell nods his head slowly and sits back down. He goes on to describe the state of Carys' home – the upstairs in particular was a mess. He did not know whether Carys liked to keep a clean home or not, but this did not look like a case of bad housekeeping. Books appeared to be thrown, a lamp table and chair were toppled over – it was clearly the scene of a struggle.

Darrell remembers thinking that earlier, when he was surveying the upstairs of the home, how Carys was such a brave woman indeed - although he does not share this with Diane. He could almost clearly picture this 63-year-old woman fighting for her own life, drawing energy from her resilient spirit, not her partially frail body. Judging from her bedclothes, it did appear she was having a nap before she was assaulted and killed. What a nightmare she awoke to.

"So you think our Carys was pushed off the balcony to her death?" asks Diane.

"Well no," says Darrell tentatively. "Are you sure you want to hear this?"

Diane adamantly nods.

Darrell explains that he had been talking to Dr. Jackson. Although he had found shallow stab wounds on Carys' abdomen and arms, the medical examiner determined the cause of death to be blunt force trauma to the head.

"Was that sustained from the fall?" asks Diane.

"No… it looks like she was already dead – being thrown over the balcony was just the murderer's attempt to make it look like an accident… or suicide."

Darrell goes on to reveal that he's quite sure he and his sergeants found the murder weapon. They found a grab-rail, meant to be installed on the bathroom wall, in Carys' bedroom. It had traces of her blood and hair on it.

Diane gasps. Carys had just bought some grab rails to have installed in her upstairs bathroom. Carys had said they were to help her on her "less energetic days." Apparently, Richard was going to install them but hadn't gotten around to it yet.

"Richard…" whispers Diane to herself.

"Sorry Diane, did you say something?" asks Darrell.

Diane shakes her head. "You know, I only heard her scream once," she says, changing the subject. "I assumed she screamed when she fell. If only I had heard her before that… if I had known she was being attacked, I would have been there. I could have stopped it."

Darrell smiles gently. "Diane it's not your fault. There is nothing you could have done differently to change this. All of your neighbours report the same thing: they only heard one scream, if anything at all. And you did not hesitate when you heard that scream. You ran right there. That's a true friend in my books!"

The inspector says his goodbyes and tells Diane he'll be by in the morning to pick her up.

Lying in bed that night, a constant thought keeps Diane from sleeping for the first hour or more. *Did Carys make that dreadful scream a split second before she was fatally whacked on the head?*

By the time Darrell arrives to pick up Diane, she has already had three cups of tea, done two loads of laundry and started cleaning the windows. This is not how Diane usually spends her Sunday mornings – she normally listens to the radio while leisurely reading the paper before diving into her writing.

But this is no ordinary Sunday. They are heading to the bank of her recently departed friend who has left (*who? them?*) a clue (*for what? to help bring clarity as to who was after her? to who wanted her dead?*).

Before Darrell even has time to exit his Range Rover to knock on Diane's front door, she has already slammed her door shut and is waiting outside the passenger door to his vehicle.

"So you're a morning person!" says Darrell jovially.

"You could say that."

Leaving Apple Mews, they drive over the metal bridge constructed above the river. Darrell would much prefer sitting next to a river, fishing with his father's mates like he had originally planned for today. But he would never be able to enjoy himself, knowing that there is a potentially strong lead that needed to be looked into immediately.

"How are you coping?" he asks Diane.

"*The emotional qualities are antagonistic to clear reasoning,*" she says, putting on a slight smile.

"And who said that?" asks Darrell.

"Sherlock Holmes," she says, smiling a tad brighter.

When they arrive at Carys' bank in Shrewsbury, Sergeant Webster and a man, wearing a grey business suit along with a grimace, are waiting for them outside.

"Someone does not look too happy with being called here on a Sunday," Darrell chuckles.

"I'm impressed you arranged this so quickly," says Diane.

They exit the Range Rover and Sergeant Webster introduces them to the bank manager whose scowl quickly disappears whilst standing next to the much taller and fitter Inspector Crothers. Darrell hands the bank manager a warrant indicating their authority to open Carys' safety deposit box.

"Right, this way," the manager says. They follow him inside, behind the counter and to the back of the bank. He unlocks a door to the vault which reveals a room with hundreds of safety deposit boxes. Diane shows him the key and tells him it should open box 2914.

The bank manager points out the corresponding box into which Diane inserts the key. She struggles for a moment to twist the key. She dries her clammy hands on her trousers and tries again. They key fits perfectly.

Diane slides the box out and places it on the table in the middle of the room.

"Wait," says Darrell, stopping Diane from opening the safety deposit box. He turns around to the bank manager and says, "Will you excuse us please?"

The same grimace from earlier returns to the manager's face, but quickly disappears again in response to Darrell's stern expression. He quickly leaves Diane, the inspector, and sergeant to their own devices.

Diane steps away from the table.

"No, you go ahead Diane," Darrell encourages.

Diane slowly opens the lid to the box. Inside they find a formal-looking document.

"It looks like a deed to a house, Sir," says Sergeant Webster.

"I think you're right Bob –a house on Bardsey Island by the looks of it," says Darrell. "Now I know I've heard that name before."

"Bardsey Island... as in Bardsey apples?" asks Bob.

"That's it!" says Diane, suddenly remembering the photographs of the Celtic crosses and the seaside pasture on Carys' wall. She had told Diane the pictures were taken on Bardsey Island. "Bardsey Island is off the coast of Wales… off the Llŷn *Peninsula* to be precise."

"Look, there's something else in the box sir," says Webster.

Darrell pulls out a folded note. He opens it to read: *Find the nest in the oak tree. A treasure awaits you.*

"Well, the way I see it, we have no other choice," says Darrell. "Diane, you and I must head to Bardsey Island immediately to find this house, and hopefully the treasure!"

Darrell would be kidding himself if he believed his enthusiasm was driven as much or more by the excitement of a scavenger hunt, and to discover a rugged land he had not yet explored.

"But sir, are you sure it's a good idea to bring…" whispers Webster, pointing his head towards Diane. "Do you really want to involve her aga—"

"I'd love to go!" cheers Diane. "So long as we can bring Rufus too!"

"Rufus comes too," replies Darrell. "Let me just make a call to the Welsh police and fill them in."

"That's very courteous of you, Inspector," says Diane.

Diane picks up the phone and dials Darrell's number. They had both gone to their respective homes to pack up some belongings to bring on their journey to Bardsey Island.

"Hello Darrell? I'm just reading here about Bardsey Island. Apparently travel to the island can be quite treacherous and boat trips can be cancelled if the winds and sea currents are too strong."

"Look Diane, I do not want you to feel uncomfortable or make you feel like you're in danger. I'm quite capable of going on my own if you would prefer not to go. I will understand."

"No, not at all! I would not miss this for the world. All I was going to say is that they recommend wrapping any bags you have in plastic to waterproof them, and to bring clothing for all types of weather. Oh, and I am going to make some sandwiches and pack some snacks, just in case food deliveries haven't been made to the island recently."

"I thought we might only stay one night. How long are you planning on staying?" Darrell laughs.

"Oh, that reminds me… when you pick me up, can we stop by Carys' to pick up Rufus' food and belongings? Do you still have access to the home?"

"Of course! See you soon."

Diane takes out a box of cellophane and starts to wrap her backpack. Before ripping the plastic, she shakes her head at herself. *You're just being silly Diane.* She decides to put some of the bag's contents – her camera in particular – in plastic bags instead. The backpack is made of a waterproof material in any case.

She opens the closet and takes out her insulated rain jacket, an article of clothing she's worn many times on hikes with Albert and on solo ramblings.

"Rufus," she calls. "I have an extra rain jacket if you'd like it."

Rufus runs up to her feet. She wraps him in the windbreaker, prompting the dog to give her a confused look.

"It's a tad too big, isn't it boy?" giggles Diane. "You can hide under my coat if the weather becomes too wild."

When Darrell arrives, he and Diane slowly walk up to Carys' home. Diane intentionally leaves Rufus at hers, sensing it would simply be too cruel to bring him to his former home without his owner – his mum – being there.

Darrell inserts a key into the front door and they enter. Diane cautiously walks towards the kitchen and stops at the entryway to the living room, half expecting to see Carys. The floor is bare of any trace that her friend had been lying there, dead, just yesterday.

In the kitchen, Diane finds Rufus' bag of food, bowl and one of his favourite bones. Her eyes are drawn to a small bookcase standing next to the kitchen table. One book stands out among the collection of cookbooks: *Bardsey Island Legends*. Diane swipes it from the shelf and heads back to the front door.

Seeing Darrell is not there waiting for her in the foyer, Diane quietly sets the things down and turns towards the staircase. Creeping up the first step and then the second, she thinks to herself, *Do I really want to see where Carys was killed?*

"Ready to go Diane?" Darrell calls.

Diane jumps, nearly tripping over the next step. She turns slowly to see Darrell standing at the bottom of the stairs.

"Yes," says Diane meekly, thinking, *at least he doesn't look cross.*

Darrell picks up the bag of food and the other items, eyeing the book curiously.

Standing outside while Darrell locks up, Diane hears what sounds like rummaging in one of Carys' bushes. She takes a few steps closer to realize it is Richard trying to escape the clutches of the branches and leaves.

"Richard! What are you doing here?" screams Diane.

Richard falls out of the bush and quickly stands up, his face a deep shade of red.

"Calm down Diane," says Darrell evenly. "Richard, is there something I can help you with?"

"No... no... no," says Richard. "Nobody can help!"

"Did you lose something chap?" Darrell tries again.

"No, I just wanted to..." says Richard, his voice trailing off.

"Sorry?" says Darrell, trying not to agitate the man.

"I just wanted to come round one last time... you know... to say goodbye like."

"I can understand that Richard," says the inspector. "Why don't you take all the time you need in the garden here. But don't go inside, okay? It's still a crime scene."

Richard nods his head. He goes to the bench and sits down, then closes his eyes, oblivious to Darrell and Diane still standing there.

"Don't they say that certain killers like to return to the scene of the crime?" asks Diane as they walk back to her house. "And are you sure you can trust him not to go inside... and fiddle with some evidence?"

"Diane, he gave me his key to the house yesterday. Plus we've installed a few CCTV cameras inside the home just in case anybody goes in... for suspicious purposes."

Diane realizes she's letting her emotions get too involved with this case. It's understandable considering who the murder victim is, but if she wants to be of some assistance to find out who killed Carys Jones, she needs to try and remain objective. That being said, Richard cannot necessarily be ruled out as a suspect.

Diane gathers her gear and Rufus, and they jump in Darrell's Range Rover. He starts the engine and therefore their three-hour drive to Porth Meudwy to catch the ferry to Bardsey Island.

Opening up the book she found at Carys', Diane reads silently for several minutes.

"Wow, it looks like we're heading to a magical and sacred place," says Diane. "This book says Bardsey

Island is the resting place for 20,000 Saints, not to mention King Arthur and Merlin the Magician!"

"Is that so?" says Darrell playfully.

"And it was a place of pilgrimage too. Apparently three treks to Bardsey equalled one to Rome!"

Completely serious this time, Darrell says, "What legends and mysteries are waiting for us there?"

Chapter 4

Darrell had parked his Range Rover close to the Porth Meudwy cove. He and Diane are a tad early for the crossing to Bardsey Island. There is no scheduled trip today, but the Welsh police arranged for Old Cai Jernigan to take them across. The captain agreed so long as he could go to his choir practice first – he hated missing his weekly session of a capella song.

To pass the time, Diane, Rufus and Darrell have plenty to keep their eyes occupied. Historic farm buildings easily entice them to imagine the hardships and pleasures of days gone by. They walk up a hill to see a stunning view of the cove and sea cliffs. A crab fisherman is slowly motoring towards the dock.

Rufus suddenly pulls his leash and swiftly runs out of sight. Diane runs after him with Darrell leisurely following behind. As Diane nears, she can hear Rufus' unrelenting barking – it has a very distressing tone. The wind blows her grey locks over her eyes, making her ears more in tune with the constant *thump-thump-thump* sound coming from the same direction as Rufus' cries.

She moves her hair out of her eyes and screams. Darrell runs up to keep Diane from planting her face in the field. He follows Diane's horrified eyes to see a wooden frame. Something is hanging from its top beam and banging against the upright to the beat of the sharp winds. That *something...* is it human?

"Rufus! Come here!" Diane yells.

But Rufus is unrelenting and refuses to leave his post next to the scaffold. Diane and Darrell walk slowly towards the dog and the source of his agitation. Diane stares at the back of the black cloak the hanging something - or *someone* - is wearing. She wills herself to take a look and find out what is swinging from these makeshift gallows. She mutters under her breath – *1-2-3* – and hops to get in front of the mystery being.

"*AAAAaaaaaaaagggggghhhh!*"

"What is it Diane?" says Darrell, rushing to stand beside her.

They both gaze at what is clearly a scarecrow with a wooden face painted to resemble that of a coyote with vicious, sharp teeth. Darrell and Diane burst out laughing, causing Rufus to bark even louder.

"Silly that I screamed," Diane giggles. "I can see why this figure made you alarmed, dear Rufus."

"Gallows Field!" shouts a voice from behind.

Diane jumps. She and Darrell turn around to see a man with a thick grey beard. The wrinkles under his eyes surely have plenty of stories to tell.

"Fed up I am of those kids ditching school and doing things like this! They're going to scare the tourists away," continues the strange man.

"You mentioned Gallows Field…" says Diane.

"Aye, there is a place not too far from here that was called Gallows Field a long time ago. A head monk from Bardsey would see to it that the murderers and robbers would meet their maker being hung there. I suppose these rascals are learning something from their school books if they're recreating a local legend…."

The man leans on his cane and looks at the discomfort in Diane's face. "Sorry, we don't need to be talking about this today. We'll be leaving for Bardsey now, in a minute. I just need to fuel up."

"Oh, are you the captain of the boat to Bardsey Island?" asks Darrell.

"Aye, the name's Cai Jernigan," he says, turning around to walk to the dock. Despite the limp in his right leg, Darrell and Diane have to pick up their pace to keep up with the local boatman.

On board, Diane can still hear the *thump-thump-thump* of the faux-hanged man. Just for a moment, she allows herself to imagine that it is Carys' killer who is hanging from the noose. She quickly forces the macabre thought from her mind as the boat enters the choppy waves.

Both she and Rufus howl in delight at the fun of the 'water rollercoaster ride.'

"And this is a tidy day compared to most," says Captain Cai of the conditions.

"Have you been taking people to the island for many years?" asks Darrell.

"Aye, a tidy spell," says the captain. Over the roar of the engine and the waves, Diane and Darrell can faintly hear him start to sing: *Mi sydd fachgen ieuanc ffôl. Yn byw yn ôl fy ffansi...*

After Rufus called their attention to two seals swimming near the boat, they arrive at Bardsey Island. Captain Cai, much spryer than he appears, unloads their overnight bags and even lifts Diane to shore.

Anticipating that Diane and Darrell are probably all set for a late lunch, the captain walks them up to a working farm and knocks on the farmhouse door.

"Deris, *S'mae!*" exclaims Cai to the older woman opening the door.

"*S'mae!*" she says, happy to see her long-time friend.

The captain introduces them to Deris Williams who helps run the farm with her husband and son, and who still takes in weary travellers in need of some sustenance. She's lived all of her 81 years on the island.

Darrell and Diane say their goodbyes and thank the captain, who reminds them that he'll come back for them this time tomorrow. Although anxious to find the house and the treasure Carys' safety deposit box is leading them to, the two sleuths are more than happy to sit at Mrs. Williams' table and enjoy some of her hearty *cawl* and homemade biscuits. It's also an excellent opportunity to get some answers from a local. Mrs. Williams even facilitates the line of questioning.

"What brings you to Bardsey Island?" she asks.

"I'm sorry to say, we're investigating the death of Carys Jones," says Diane. "Did you know her?"

"God bless her," says Mrs. Williams' solemnly.

"So you knew her then?" asks Darrell.

"Aye. Not well mind you. She was a quiet character, but always pleasant."

Mrs. Williams goes on to say that Carys owned a nice house over the hill that overlooks the sea and the beach below.

"I don't know why, but people call it *The Oak Tree House*. I *atto* laugh the first time I heard it because my name, Deris, means oak tree… that's what my Nain taught me anyhow."

"Deris is a lovely name," comments Diane. "So *The Oak Tree House,* they call it."

Diane looks knowingly at Darrell, each remembering the clue – about the nest in the oak tree – that was also found in the safety deposit box.

"Does anybody live in the house now, Mrs. Williams?" Darrell asks.

"No, I dare say not. There were some mainlanders renting it – two artists they said they were. But it's been empty ever since last Autumn, I think… my memory is not as good as it once was."

"I can relate!" laughs Diane. "Our dear, young Darrell here has not been hit with such afflictions… yet."

"Thanks for your time and for a delicious lunch, Mrs. Williams. We must be off," Darrell says.

"Come give us a *cwtch*," says Mrs. Williams, running up to each of them to give them a warm hug. "Oh, I have a treat for Rufus – I'll find it sharpish!" The farmer runs into the pantry and comes out carrying a large bone. "It's from one of our cattle, and there's still a little meat on there for *youer* Rufus!" she muses.

After promising they would be back if they were "sinking for some tea," Darrell and Diane set out in the direction Mrs. Williams had pointed out – the way to *The*

Oak Tree House. Rufus eventually follows, after taking some time to gnaw on his new goody.

Over the hill, they see a single house overlooking the water below. The view is stunning: the green still rich in the surrounding fields, a blue sky with generous white clouds, a lively sea crashing into the island's rocks and a series of kittiwakes and razorbills in flight. Off in the distance, Diane even sees the lighthouse and perhaps, just perhaps, a trace of ancient ruins. She can see why Carys was attracted to this isolated paradise, although she herself would perhaps get lonely after a time – especially during this time of year. Apple Mews, with its "overly concerned" neighbours, must have been a culture shock to Carys at first.

They find *The Oak Tree House* closed and secured as any rental property on the island would be during the non-tourist season. Luckily, along with the deed and the note, there was also a set of keys they found in the safety deposit box. Darrell takes the keys out of his pocket and for a half-second has to hope that these keys do in fact belong to Carys' former home.

The first key Darrell tries does not fit in the keyhole, but the second does and even turns to let them into the house. Diane almost gasps upon walking into the property's impressive foyer at the bottom of a grand staircase. Carys had lived in a very nice home in Apple

Mews, but Diane had never imagined that her friend owned such a luxurious – or, as the Welsh say, tidy! – place.

The inspector and Diane split up, with Rufus choosing to stay in the foyer to concentrate on his bone. Diane enters the sitting room, half expecting to see Carys' knitting projects or a stack of leaflets seeking donations and volunteers for the homeless. Instead, Diane finds herself on a historical home tour, except there are no cordons stopping her from touching the stone surround of the fireplace, or from lifting the white sheets off the leather armchairs and hand-carved coffee table.

As they tour room to room, Diane and Darrell get the sense that everything is in its proper place; and, aside from the sheets covering all of the furniture, the property appears just like a picture-perfect display home would in a new residential development.

Naturally, when Carys moved, she would have taken all her belongings, but the house feels so unoccupied, so unlived in, that every time Darrell opens a drawer or feels at the top of a bookcase nothing is to be found. He is starting to wonder whether this trip may have been a waste of time. Maybe Carys' note is not meant to be interpreted as a clue.

Still, Darrell cannot shake the feeling that when she wrote the note - *Find the nest in the oak tree. A treasure awaits you* - she meant for someone on the right side of the law, such as himself, to be the recipient, and to direct them to *something* crucial. A something, he suspects, that Carys did not want the killer to find.

Still, Darrell hasn't noticed an oak tree or any trees surrounding the house. Since the home is nicknamed *The Oak Tree House*, perhaps the "nest" is hiding somewhere inside the property.

In one of the bedrooms upstairs, Darrell climbs the ladder to the loft. His children, Jeremy and Chloe, would love sleeping up here, he thinks. He looks under the bed and knocks on the walls to hear if he can detect any secret passageways. *You've watched too many adventure movies with the kids, Darrell.*

Darrell looks up to see a cord hanging from the ceiling. He pulls on it gently, and then uses a little more muscle, to slowly releases a ladder which presumably leads to an attic. Darrell takes out his torch and holds it in his mouth as he climbs up into the highest section of the home.

Inside the attic Darrell can stand, but only in a hunched-back position. He shines the torch around the room and finds it, disappointingly, uncluttered. Still, there are a few boxes in the middle of the room. He puts on some gloves and gets to work searching for anything "nest-like" or that may have a connection to Carys Jones.

Yet all Darrell finds in the boxes are Christmas ornaments, some sherry glasses and some old vinyl records. He searches through each item carefully looking for bits of paper that might be tucked inside, even for clues hidden among the song titles. But nothing seems to be linked to a nest or treasure or to Carys Jones.

He switches off his torch and turns to head back towards the light coming from the bedroom from whence he came. As he's about to climb down the ladder, Darrell stops - he hears movement behind him.

Darrell wonders if it is a squirrel, though it sounds too loud to be. Perhaps it is a rat or a gull, or even a fox. Darrell knows foxes are not normally a threat to humans, but who knows how one might react if it feels like it's being backed into a corner of a relatively small space?

Darrell's curiosity gets the better of him and he walks, quietly, towards the sound.

When he feels like he's just close enough, he quickly turns on his torch. What he sees makes him jolt back and grip his chest – and it makes the object in his sights shriek!

"Diane, what are you doing up here?!?!"

"Darrell, you startled me!"

"I could say the same thing about you. What are you doing up here roaming around in the dark?"

"I was trying to find the light switch…."

They both burst out into laughter, relieved they came across each other and not something more… sinister.

"How did you get up here anyway?"

"I climbed a ladder from the master bedroom," explains Diane.

"Okay, I'll meet you down there. I've looked at everything up here, and there's no sign of a nest or treasure."

Darrell shines the torch so Diane can find the ladder she had climbed up, then climbs down his.

In the master bedroom, Diane starts searching through the dresser. All of the drawers are empty except for one with postcards. She flips them over to see they are still blank. *That's no fun,* she thinks, although one looks awfully similar to one of the photographs still hanging in Carys' Apple Mews home.

Now in the master room too, Darrell opens the wardrobe only to find a handful of hangers and a layer of dust on the bottom.

Diane – distracted by the lustrous sunrays, particularly vibrant for this time of year – looks outside. She stops what she is doing and walks to the bed. She then lies down on top of the large white sheet covering the mattress and duvet.

Noticing immediately that Diane is no longer standing, Darrell rushes to 'her bedside'.

"Diane, are you alright? I can take you back to the rental cottage if you would like to take a rest."

Giggling, Diane stands up immediately as if nothing is the matter with her, body and soul.

"Now just trust me," says Diane, still giggling. "I want you to lie down, right where I was, and to look out the window."

"Are you having a laugh?"

"I promise Darrell, this is pertinent to the case," says Diane, more seriously this time.

Grumbling to himself, the inspector complies and lies down on the bed. He takes a moment to look outside the window. As soon as his eyes zero in on the object

Diane is surely meaning for him to see, Darrell bursts into laughter and bolts up from the bed.

"You miserable old woman!" he exclaims, rushing out of the room and down the stairs. Diane resumes her guffawing. She cannot remember the last time she's laughed this much, but is glad her years have not stolen her youthful spirit.

Darrell swings open the front door, which finally makes Rufus release his bone. He and Diane both chase after the inspector around to the other side of the house.

Darrell stops under an oak tree that must be at least 100 years old. They would not have seen the tree when they arrived at the house since they were coming from the other direction.

Diane gazes up at the long, wise, leafy branches, some of which extend so they provide shade to the inside of the master bedroom. One of the branches appears to have a round deformation, an enlarged knot perhaps, or a bur. She stares at it further to realize its texture looks softer, its appearance a little more haphazard than tree bark. Whatever it is, it is quite camouflaged among the branches and sticks.

"Darrell, do you suppose that looks like a nest?" Diane asks.

The inspector stares up to where Diane is pointing for a good minute. He nods his head. He notices that the branch the nest is on also lines up with the master bedroom's window.

"I think you're right, Diane Dimbleby. And was it just me, or was there something coming from that branch that was blinding?"

Diane agrees that in retrospect, lying on the bed, it did seem that something from where the nest is located was so scintillating. It is their amazingly good fortune that they were in the master bedroom at this very time of day when the sun would shine and reflect off this... this... whatever this is... perfectly to capture their attention.

"We need to find out what is in that nest!" Diane says adamantly.

As Diane attempts to jump and grip the branch lowest to the ground, Darrell runs to the garden shed and fortuitously finds a ladder inside. He would have been willing to scale up the tree trunk and then climb branch by branch like he did many a time as a child, but, being a little rusty, he's relieved to find the apparatus.

With Diane still attempting to jump to a branch, Darrell sets the ladder up against the tree and asks her to hold it steady. Still being in prime athletic shape, Darrell quickly and effortlessly climbs up the ladder and then the branches that rise up beyond the last rung. He then pulls himself up to sit on the thick branch where the nest is resting.

"What do you see?!" Diane calls out with Rufus barking beside her.

"I see a wire mesh!"

"A wire mesh!?! That's it???" Diane yells. "Or is it to protect the treasure underneath perhaps!?! Protect it from birds and other predators?"

Ignoring Diane's line of inquiry, Darrell carefully removes the fine mesh. His eyes widen. He stares at what is before him in shock. He then carefully grabs a glove from his pocket and picks the object up.

It is the most splendid diamond ring he has ever seen – and that's including the ones he's seen in adverts. *This indeed could be a motive for murder.*

Darrell carefully places the ring in his pocket. Although the pocket is zippered, Darrell does not hastily climb down the tree like how he climbed up. Diane is still holding the base of the ladder when his feet touch the ground.

This time, Rufus, with his eager bark, is the first to ask Darrell what he found.

"I need to find out where it came from and how much it's worth..." says the inspector to himself.

"Of what? You need to find out the value and provenance of what!?!" asks Diane restlessly.

Darrell unzips his pocket and reveals the treasure that he found in the nest of the oak tree on Bardsey Island.

Diane gasps and is silent for several seconds. "That's incredible!" she finally says, admiring the gorgeous diamond radiating in the afternoon sun.

Walking to their rental cottage, Diane and Darrell agree that they better not tell the few people they might run into on the island about the diamond ring. In fact, they decide that after they place the jewel securely inside Diane's portable lock box – something she wisely packed among the rain gear and snacks – they will not talk of the jewel again until they are safely back in Apple Mews.

Chapter 5

They arrive at the cottage in silence; both Diane and Darrell are lost in thought. There is much to think about. How long has the diamond ring been hiding in the oak tree? Did Carys hide it herself? Who else knew about the diamond ring? Was the diamond the killer's motive for murder?

Diane knows they have no choice, but she would really like to head back home right away instead of staying the night. There's a murder to solve... her close friend's murder. Still, from the outside, the cottage looks quite charming with its slate roof, its bright green door and with the smoke invitingly coming out of the chimney.

But why is there a fire going when they hadn't been to the cottage yet? Diane nudges Darrell and points to the smoky plume floating up into the sky. Darrell nods his head. He carefully walks to the closest window and peers inside.

"Do you see someone?" Diane whispers.

Darrell shakes his head. He starts to walk to the next window and then stops suddenly when a voice starts to sing:

♪Dear Blackbird, I'll list why thou singest. My harp for awhile shall be still…♪

"I believe I recognize that voice," says Diane.

"I believe I do as well," says Darrell with a knock on the door.

Captain Cai Jernigan stops singing and opens the door.

"I didn't expect to see you still on the island," says Diane, laughing.

"Aye, I didn't think I'd be 'ere so long either!" Cai says with a twinkle in his eye. "Deris asked me to see that everything was in working order here for youer. I had to get some new lamps and matches, but she's tidy now."

"So you're the ferry captain and Bardsey's hospitality agent as well… is there anything you don't do?" Diane says with a wink.

"My lady, I wasn't brought up under a tub, that's for certain!" says the captain. "I must be going now before the sun goes to sleep."

Captain Cai starts off towards the ferry. Diane and Darrell both stare after him for a moment and then turn to each other. "Hadn't we better get back?" they both say at the same time.

"Oh, Captain Cai!" Diane yells. "Wait for us!"

After dropping Diane and Rufus back home in Apple Mews, Darrell decides he better head to the station for a little while, even though it's a Sunday night. It's better for him to place the diamond ring in evidence right away.

"Good evening Julia," Darrell says to the desk sergeant as he walks into the station.

"Oh sir, I'm glad you're here," says the desk sergeant. "There's a lady here waiting for you. She's been here all day. We've told her you weren't in Shrewsbury today, but she still insisted on staying. I expect she would have stayed the whole night if she had to."

"Did she say what she wanted?"

"She says it's about Carys Jones. She's in the visitors' lounge."

"Thank you, Julia."

Double-checking the diamond ring is still safely secured in his pocket, Darrell heads to the visitors' lounge. Inside he sees a frail-looking woman – not overly elderly though, possibly in her 60s – sipping coffee. Although she's apparently been there all day, her eyes look as alert and determined as if she has just arrived.

Before Darrell can even get a word in, she stands and says, "You must be Inspector Crothers!"

"Yes I —"

"I'm sorry to intrude on your Sunday, but I thought it important that I have a word with you before you go any further with your investigation of Carys Jones' death."

"Oh? And what is your interest in the case, Mrs. ..."

"Mrs. Thomas, Mrs. Rosalyn Thomas," the woman responds. "I heard about Carys' death on the news late last night. Carys Jones was my cousin, you see."

Darrell stares at the woman for at least a minute, maybe two. He's tired and being in this state, he feels like he's more apt to miss any cues revealing the woman is a sham. It wouldn't be the first time someone came forward falsely claiming to be a relative of a deceased person. It happens for a number of reasons, usually greedy ones. There was also that time a sick bloke came in pretending he was the son of a victim, just so he could view a corpse "in the flesh."

Darrell shudders at the thought. "Is that so?" he says finally responding to Mrs. Thomas' statement.

"Aye," the woman tells him. "Carys and I grew up together in Wales, in Aberystwyth... she was only a few years older than me, and we did everything together. It was like we were sisters... best friends really."

What Mrs. Thomas did not say, or even bring herself to admit, is that she had always been a tad jealous of Carys. Carys had good looks and lots of friends and was popular with the boys. Rosalyn's mother would always say things like, "Now why can't you be as helpful as Carys around the house?" or, "Isn't Carys' voice just beautiful?" Even when Carys became a graphic designer, everyone gushed about how exciting her career was. Still, Mrs. Thomas liked to think she came to terms with her jealousy long ago. She had raised a wonderful son, and sure, her career hadn't been as glamorous as Carys', but she had still worked as a bank teller for many years. Plus, she and Carys had shared many fond memories in childhood too.

"Had you seen Mrs. Jones recently?" Darrell asks.

"No." Mrs. Thomas explains that Carys married when she was very young. She had met this wealthy entrepreneur, a lot older than she, but they genuinely seemed madly in love. They moved to Bardsey Island and seemed to enjoy their life there. Carys would sometimes write Mrs. Thomas letters telling her about the isolating but magical winters and exciting summers there on the island. But when her husband passed away, Carys felt she could not keep on living in the house they had once shared. That's why she ended up moving away from Bardsey to Apple Mews. Mrs. Thomas adds that she hasn't seen Carys since she left Wales and they hadn't written many letters to each other.

What Mrs. Thomas is not comfortable admitting to the inspector, however, is that about six months ago she wrote to Carys asking if she could borrow some money. Mrs. Thomas had been having some financial problems after some bad investments, an honest mistake of course.

"Thank you for telling me about Carys' background, Mrs. Thomas," the inspector says. "It's very helpful for our inquiry. And I'm truly sorry for your loss. We knew Carys had no children; we hadn't been able to track down any relatives yet."

"I'm her closest living relative," says Mrs. Thomas. "So I thought it important for me to be here—"

"To help find the person responsible?"

"Oh yes Inspector, of course, that's a given! And also for the reading of the will – I didn't want to hold up that process."

In cases like these, Darrell had observed it to be quite common for certain family members to be focused on the possibility of a valuable inheritance rather than the passing of their so-called loved one. It's a cruel occurrence, but hardly surprising.

"Mrs. Thomas, up to now I have no knowledge of Mrs. Jones having a will," says Darrell, "but I shall inform you as soon as I have more information about whether a will exists or not."

"But surely everyone has a will," says Mrs. Thomas.

Darrell shoots her a stern look, convincing Mrs. Thomas that she has taken up more than enough of his time. After she leaves, Darrell shakes his head. He feels bad that Carys' closest relation is so money-hungry. Still, desperation can take away a person's manners, and it's possible Mrs. Thomas is in desperate need of some cash. But he cannot focus on helping Mrs. Thomas' financial situation right now – he had a murder to solve.

Still, she had been helpful. Carys' late husband had probably bought Carys the expensive ring and also left her with a sizeable inheritance if the husband was in fact as wealthy as Mrs. Thomas described. Money may have been the killer's motive.

Had the murderer also raided a secret stash of notes or jewels in Carys' home after killing her? It didn't appear that way, but if the killer knew where she kept her valuables, he could have taken them without making a mess.

Before leaving the visitors' lounge, Darrell notices Mrs. Thomas' plastic coffee cup. He picks it up and throws it in the bin. Walking down the hallway, he stops and thinks: *Everyone is a suspect at this point.* He returns to the lounge and takes the cup out of the bin. He doubts Mrs. Thomas committed the murder – her biggest fault is probably wanting to cash in on her cousin's death – but just to be sure he will drop the cup off to the forensics lab for analysis.

Just to cover all his bases he should get Sergeant Webster to run a background check on Mrs. Thomas too – the sergeant is always incredibly thorough. But it's Sunday night, so he won't disturb him now. He sits at the sergeant's desk and writes him a note asking him to run the check first thing Monday.

After dropping the coffee cup off to the lab, Darrell heads to the evidence locker. He looks over his shoulder to see if anyone is present before he takes the diamond ring out of his pocket. He does not think any corrupt officers work out of Shrewsbury – in that way the force is exceptional – but when a diamond this size is present, who knows who may be tempted to turn crooked. After locking up the ring and the other items they retrieved from Bardsey Island, Darrell heads back out of the station, wishing the desk sergeant a good night.

Anxious to get home and kiss each of his kids and his wife, something stops him from going into his Range

Rover – that uncomfortable but knowing feeling of being watched.

Darrell bends down and pretends to tie his shoe while surreptitiously looking around. Then he sees her, about 60 feet away. It's Mrs. Thomas parked across the street, and she is definitely watching him.

"Is there something else, Mrs. Thomas?" Darrell shouts.

Mrs. Thomas quickly looks elsewhere, turns on the engine and drives away.

Darrell wonders what the woman really wants. *The diamond, probably,* he thinks. Being once very close to Carys, she must know about it. It had probably been her cousin's wedding ring. And now Mrs. Thomas must think she's bound to inherit it. The inspector will find out more about Mrs. Thomas' financial situation after Sergeant Webster runs the background check tomorrow.

Inside his Range Rover, before Darrell turns the key in the ignition, he thinks of Diane. He suddenly realizes that it may not be safe for Diane to be alone with the killer at large, especially because her curiosity generally veers her towards, and not away from, danger. Darrell had made a near-fatal mistake when Diane was left to her own devices on a previous case. He will never forgive himself for Diane getting kidnapped and nearly killed by the so-called "Sergeant Benedek."

Darrell takes out his phone and quickly dials Diane's number.

"Hello?"

"Hello, Diane… Darrell here… where are you?"

"Why Inspector Crothers, do you miss me already?" she giggles.

"Diane, seriously, where are you?"

"I'm just taking Rufus for a walk around the village green. Then we're going to the pub for a late supper."

"Diane, I'm ordering you to go home this instant and to lock all of your doors and windows."

Diane cracks up laughing. She doesn't remember the last time she's locked her door. Plus she's a grown woman, old enough to be the inspector's mum.

"What's gotten into you Darrell?" she asks, still laughing.

"I just think you're probably the most vulnerable person connected to the case right now. The killer is still at large and might very well know that you've been helping me with the investigation. I know you're a force to be reckoned with, but you still could be in danger. Plus, you're one of Carys' closest friends."

Darrell then goes on to tell Diane about Mrs. Thomas and how he feels like there's something fishy about her.

"Do you think she's responsible for Carys' death?" asks Diane, no longer laughing.

"No. I have a feeling she's just waiting to see what Carys left her in her will… if there is a will. Had Carys ever mentioned she had a cousin Rosalyn from Aberystwyth?"

"No, I never heard her talk of any cousins," says Diane, walking Rufus back to the cottage. "Are you sure she's telling the truth about being Carys' relative?"

Diane reminds Darrell that anybody could pretend to be a sister or cousin or uncle or son. It would be quite easy for that someone to find out information about marriages, deaths and places of residence, especially when it came to high-profile individuals like wealthy entrepreneurs.

"Though if she is just pretending to be a cousin, I wonder under what pretext she was able to ascertain all of this information," Diane thinks aloud.

"We will be running a background check first thing tomorrow morning, and we should be able to confirm whether or not this woman is, in fact, Mrs. Rosalyn

Thomas," says Darrell. "Now go straight home and lock all the doors."

"I will. Good night Darrell."

"Good night."

Darrell's mind drifts back to Mrs. Thomas' glare he had witnessed just a few minutes ago. For a split second, he thinks that maybe this woman is putting on an act, but what the *act* is he cannot be certain of right now.

Driving away from the police station, Mrs. Thomas feels anger creep through her shoulders and back. Her face feels flush, and her head is beginning to ache. She needs to calm down.

She pulls over to the side of the road and turns off her engine. She closes her eyes and attempts to calm her breathing. *Of course Carys has a will, who doesn't have a will? They just haven't found it yet. It will all work out.*

Mrs. Thomas thinks back to the relaxation audiobook she had borrowed from the library. The instructor on the CD had said to visualize a beautiful place. Mrs. Thomas closes her eyes and visualizes the tropical island that she wishes to live on. The sunset over the crashing waves helps to calm her anger and anxiety every time. And if all goes to plan, this tropical place of serenity will soon become a reality.

Richard is tossing and turning in bed. Unsurprisingly, he has not been able to sleep since Saturday.

He gets up and goes to the kitchen. He checks all the bottles on the counter to see if any have any drops of beer or whisky left. Richard rarely drinks, perhaps a pint on his birthday, but this weekend is far from orthodox.

One of the bottles is still half-filled with ale. He chugs it despite the beer being unappetizingly warm. He sets the bottle down on the counter so hard that it smashes in his hand.

"Bloody hell!" he shouts.

Richard runs to the bathroom and unrolls a wad of toilet paper to wrap around his bleeding hand. He stares at the red soaking through the outermost layer of the tissue and then looks straight in the mirror at the bags under his eyes.

"You are a bad person," he says to himself over and over again.

♠ ♠ ♠ ♠ ♠ ♠

The next morning, Darrell leaves home before the children are even out of bed. He's only done that a handful of times in the past. Even though it's early, when he arrives at the station he finds the forensic report waiting for him on his desk.

"Note to self, I owe the whole forensic lab a round at the pub," Darrell thinks.

Before he even takes a sip of his coffee, Darrell starts reading. According to the fingerprint analyst, two sets of prints were found on Mrs. Thomas coffee cup. One set belongs to him, which makes sense because he hadn't been wearing gloves when he removed the cup from the bin.

The other matches a set of prints found at Carys' Jones house.

Darrell realizes that it is almost a certainty that the woman he spoke to last night is a liar. She could have been lying about being a relative of Carys'. Or if she is, in fact, Carys' cousin, she lied about not seeing Carys after Carys left Wales. How else could she explain her prints being in Carys' Apple Mews home?

Darrell also reads in the forensic report that a sample for DNA analysis was also obtainable from the cup, but it will take a few days to compare that particular DNA with Carys Jones'.

"Good morning Bob," says Darrell to Sergeant Webster sitting at a desk on the other side of the room.

"Good morning, Sir. I got your note and am starting the background check on Rosalyn Thomas. I also left the information you asked for on Carys Jones' caregiver, Richard Butler."

"Thank you, Bob."

Darrell finds the folder on Richard and opens it. *Currently lives in Apple Mews, employed by Mrs. Carys Jones, clean criminal record, clean driving record. Former address: 128 Wilbury Lane, Shrewsbury.*

"Why do I know that address? Bob, can you look up an address for me?" Darrell asks.

"Sure thing, sir."

"Look up 128 Wilbury Lane, Shrewsbury, please."

After a minute, Sergeant Webster comes back with, "It's the address for Safe Refuge, the men's homeless shelter sir."

"A homeless shelter?"

Darrell suddenly remembers Diane telling him that Carys worked a lot with the homeless charity here in

Shrewsbury. Carys might have met Richard at the shelter, and then hired him for a proper job to get him off the street.

Yet Darrell does not like where his mind is heading. He does not like to judge a man just because he had once had a bad string of luck, but he cannot help wondering: Richard hit rock bottom once… has he again? And has he taken Carys down with him?

Chapter 6

Without letting another second pass, Darrell picks up the phone to call Diane. Although she knows about Carys' so-called cousin, the shady Mrs. Thomas, Darrell wouldn't put it past Diane to invite her in, should Mrs. Thomas come knocking at her door.

And then there's the question of Richard. Darrell is pretty sure Diane is already suspicious of the man, but if he *is* the killer, he could probably, at the very least, intimidate a woman 15 years his senior.

Darrell doesn't like to hover, but he has to make sure Diane is safe.

"Hello!" Diane answers cheerfully.

"Diane, I need you to promise me you'll stay inside, at least until I can ensure your complete safety."

"But Rufus and I couldn't resist. We just had to get outside to enjoy this beautiful day."

"You're outside right now? Bloody hell!"

"Darrell, calm down. What is it?"

Darrell has let his worry, albeit disguised by his temper, get the best of him. After counting to ten in his head – isn't that what all the experts tell a person to do to keep their wits about them? – he explains that there are two plausible suspects: Richard Butler and Rosalyn Thomas. Both could easily get to Diane, in one way or another.

"I'm not usually one to give ultimatums, but if you do not stay inside your cottage, at least for the day, I'm going to have to take Rufus to the RSPCA."

Diane bites her lip to keep from laughing – she's not used to hearing the inspector talk so sternly to her. Then it hits her: he's right. She is putting herself in a precarious position every time she steps out the door.

"Not to worry, Darrell," she says. "I'm quickly going to run to the shops to buy some doggie pee pads for Rufus. That way neither he nor I will have to leave the house for the rest of the day."

"Thank you Diane. We'll chat soon. Stay safe."

Darrell hangs up the phone and heaves a sigh of relief. He then flips open the folder on his desk that he's recently labelled 'Carys Jones'. On top, he notices a business card that says 'Henry Taylor, Solicitor.'

Darrell suddenly remembers that they haven't tracked down a possible will of Carys'. He dials the number on the card and leaves a message on the voicemail for the solicitor to call him back as soon as possible.

He looks over to see Sergeant Webster, who is on the phone and furiously taking notes.

"Find much on Mrs. Thomas, Bob?" Darrell asks after the sergeant hangs up.

"She's not as angelic as she might appear, sir."

Darrell walks over to Sergeant Webster's desk to hear what his man has found out. The sergeant tells him that he's confirmed that Mrs. Rosalyn Thomas is from Aberystwyth, Wales, and that her mother and Carys' mother were sisters.

What's more, Mrs. Thomas has a chequered past. Sergeant Webster pulls up her criminal record on his computer. Darrell immediately notices the mugshot. He's positive it belongs to the same woman he met last night. The cold glare he had witnessed while she watched him from her car is staring at him again from Sergeant Webster's computer screen.

"That's her," says Darrell confidently.

They look at her file up on the screen. A few years ago Mrs. Rosalyn Thomas had been charged with intent to commit insider trading fraud. She served a two-year community sentence where she was ordered to meet with a probation officer and a counsellor on a regular basis.

"She lives in Swansea now sir, and I was able to get hold of her bank records," says the sergeant. "When I asked the bank manager to send them over, I don't think he meant to, but he snickered on the phone."

Sergeant Webster shows Darrell the printouts from the bank. It is clear from the big, fat negative sign that Mrs. Thomas is not only broke – she's in the red.

"Thank you Bob. Now we need to figure out her movements from Swansea to here. Did she really only arrive here the day after Mrs. Jones' murder?"

"Already done, sir. She took the train from Swansea to Shrewsbury on Thursday. Then I found records that she hired a car at the railway station."

"So she arrived in Shrewsbury two days before Mrs. Jones died. I don't suppose you've located where she's been staying since she arrived?"

"She checked into a Bed & Breakfast just outside Apple Mews on Thursday night."

"Well done Bob!" Darrell shouts, slapping the sergeant sportsmanlike on the back.

After nearly choking on his coffee, Sergeant Webster looks delighted to have impressed his superior.

Darrell races to the phone on his desk and asks the operator to transfer him to the South Wales Police.

"Hello, this is Inspector Darrell Crothers from the Shrewsbury Police Force. I'd like to talk to someone who may have had dealings with a Mrs. Rosalyn Thomas of Swansea."

It just so happens that one of the inspectors who worked Mrs. Thomas' fraud case is at the station and able to take Darrell's call. The Welshman tells Darrell that he remembers Mrs. Thomas well. How did he put it? *"He has never seen someone so greedy - so in love with money – in his life."*

Talking to people who knew her, the Welsh inspector found out that apparently Mrs. Thomas was always wanting to borrow money from people and that she would always try to wiggle her way into people's lives just to have a large piece of their pie. She was a gambler too and lost lots of money, from making bad investments to making hefty bets at the casino. That's why, as part of her sentence, she was ordered to seek gambling addiction counselling.

Darrell hangs up the phone. It's clear that Mrs. Thomas is quickly climbing her way up to the top of the suspect list, but first there's something that needs to cleared up once and for all.

"Bob, thanks again! Your work is the bee's knees!" says Darrell, grabbing his coat. "I'm headed to Apple Mews to see Richard Butler."

Richard lives in a small apartment above Apple Mews' pub. Before climbing the long staircase to Richard's front door, Darrell briefly wonders if he should have called some backup.

At the top of the staircase, Darrell sees a messy pile of newspapers and leaflets littering the front stoop. He gently shoves them out of the way with his foot and knocks on the screen door. After a minute and no answer, Darrell knocks again, harder this time.

He can hear something inside and then notices one of the slats of the front window blinds move.

"Richard, it's me, Inspector Darrell Crothers. I'm sorry to bother you, but I just need to have one more chat with you… just to finalize some details. It won't take long…"

Darrell can hear the chain slide out of the lock, and the front door slowly opens. In front of him stands Richard, in an undershirt and boxer shorts; his hair is ruffled, and he clearly hasn't shaved in days. Richard holds open the door without making eye contact with the inspector, and then trudges over to the small sitting room.

Inside, Darrell's first instinct is that Richard's apartment has been ransacked. Upon closer scrutiny, however, the empty beer bottles, the clothes strewn about, and the overflowing kitchen sink all seem to indicate a man who has "let his place, and himself, go".

Richard removes a pizza box and a pair of trousers from one of the chairs so the inspector can sit. He doesn't even bother to move the heap on the couch where he's now sitting.

"I'm not going to ask how you're getting on because clearly you're going through a rough patch," Darrell says, trying to infuse his voice with compassion. "But we need to clear some things up."

"Yes," says Richard, meekly.

"First, is it true you used to live at the Safe Refuge shelter in Shrewsbury?"

Richard nods his head.

"And is that how you met Mrs. Jones?"

"Yes. I met her at the soup kitchen. She was nice to me from the get-go. We'd have all these wonderful talks. After a while, she told me she knew I was capable of holding down a job... of making a new life for myself... she hired me to be her caregiver... she believed in –" Richard stops, feeling a sob coming on. He closes his eyes and holds his breath.

"Take your time Richard," says Darrell considerately. "Now, about your accounts of what happened on Saturday—"

"You mean the day Mrs. Jones died!?" cries Richard.

"Yes, that day. It appears as though you may have got some of your facts mixed up... it's understandable. You were probably in shock..."

"It's all my fault," says Richard, now crying more explicitly.

"What do you mean by that, Richard?" asks Darrell quietly, trying to maintain some composure in the conversation.

After some minutes, when Richard is able to reach a calm state, he explains that he has been hiding something from the police. He did, in fact, arrive at Mrs. Jones' place while she was still alive. They had chatted, and before she laid down for her nap, they decided Richard would indeed make lamb casserole for her dinner.

But what Richard had been too ashamed to admit is that he had left Carys' home for a short time to go to the grocer's. He had realized he had no onions or rosemary – he didn't think the casserole would taste half as good without onions *and* rosemary.

"So when I went out to buy them ingredients, whoever must have killed Mrs. Jones did it while I was gone! And you see, I didn't lock the door when I left. So it's all my fault. I wasn't there to protect her, and I let them in."

"Richard, it's not your fault. I don't expect anyone in Apple Mews locks their doors. It's only the fault of those who committed the dirty deed. You remember that! Thank you for telling me."

For the first time in days, Richard feels a weight lift off his shoulders. It feels good to have finally "confessed his sins" to somebody.

The inspector then asks him if Mrs. Jones had even mentioned a cousin named Rosalyn Thomas.

"Oh yes, a couple of times. I remember because the day before she was talking on the phone to somebody and she seemed quite annoyed. I asked her if everything was all right… she said, 'Oh, it's just that cousin of mine… Rosalyn.' The way she said 'Rosalyn,' I could tell her cousin must be a pain in the arse!"

"Thank you Richard. You have been very helpful!"

Darrell shakes Richard's hand and rushes out the door. He is now ready to arrest Mrs. Thomas for the murder of her cousin. First though, he races over to Diane's cottage just up the road.

Diane's writing session is interrupted by an incessant knocking at her front door. Both she and Rufus run towards the sound. Then Diane stops. It's at times like this – when a murderer is lurking about – that she wishes she had a peephole in her door.

"Who is it?" she asks assertively.

"It's me… Inspector Crothers… Darrell."

"Well why didn't you say so?" she says jovially, opening the door. "Have you come to make sure Rufus and I haven't succumbed to cabin fever?"

Disregarding Diane's humour, Darrell immediately tells her that he's about to arrest Carys Jones' cousin, Rosalyn Thomas, for her murder.

"That can't be possible," says Diane adamantly.

"But there's her criminal record, she lied about being in Mrs. Jones' home, she arrived in the area two nights before the murder…."

Diane holds up her hand, which immediately stops Darrell from arguing further. She motions for the inspector to follow her up the staircase to the second floor of her home. They stop in front of a railing, one that looks remarkably similar to the one in Carys' home – the railing that Carys was thrown over.

"I'm guessing this Mrs. Rosalyn Thomas is not some bionic bodybuilder…." says Diane.

"No, not at all," laughs Darrell. "Actually, she's quite frail looking. But her beady eyes more than make up for it, I can tell you that."

"Now, can you imagine this Mrs. Thomas being able to lift Carys over the railing… even if Carys was unconscious or already dead?"

"You're probably right," says the inspector. "Unless she hides it well, Mrs. Thomas does not have enough strength do that.

Darrell's mind is whirling. He had been so sure that Mrs. Thomas was the murderer. Everything points to her: her lust for money, her demand to see Carys Jones' will, lying about not seeing Carys since their days in Wales, arriving in the area before and not after the murder….

But she couldn't have done it alone…

… she could have had help though.

"That's it! Mrs. Thomas has an accomplice!" yells Darrell. "I need to go talk to Richard again."

Darrell hurries down the stairs and out of Diane's cottage without even petting Rufus goodbye. On the way back to the apartment over the pub, Darrell looks over to see Richard sitting on a bench on the edge of the green.

"Richard!" shouts Darrell, running across the lane.

Richard looks up with a serene smile on his face. "I haven't been outside in days."

"Richard, I forgot to ask you about Mrs. Jones' other caregiver…"

"Brian?"

"Yes, that's it, Brian. You mentioned he went on holiday. Do you know where?"

"I'm not certain, but I think he said Wales. That's where he's from anyway."

"Richard, thank you! Truly!"

Darrell is quite confident he's found Mrs. Thomas' accomplice. He jogs towards his parked Range Rover and decides he's going to call in a few officers to meet him at the B&B where Mrs. Thomas has been staying. First though, he calls Diane.

"Diane, Darrell here. I think I know who the accomplice is. I want you to double check that your doors are locked and don't open the door to anyone."

"Thank you Darrell, I will."

Diane goes downstairs to re-lock the front door and checks to make sure the back door is secured too. She then heads back upstairs to resume looking for a new book to read. While going through the pile of novels on her bedroom floor, she hears a creaking noise downstairs. Must be Rufus, she thinks, until she notices him sound asleep on top of her bed.

She goes back downstairs and looks around the living room but sees nothing out of the ordinary. She looks around the kitchen and does not find anything or anyone strange either. "Perhaps the cottage is catching up with me and my creaky bones," Diane chuckles to herself.

Climbing the staircase to go back to her bedroom, Diane hears another creak, and it's louder this time.

Diane quickly turns around. A young man is walking up the stairs and heading straight towards her. Behind him, she can see a strange woman standing at the bottom of the staircase.

"Kill her now Brian!" the woman yells. "She's helping the police!"

Diane turns and runs up the remaining stairs. At the top of the staircase she meets Rufus, who charges down the steps. Without hesitation, Rufus leaps up and pushes Brian down the staircase. The young man lets out a panicked holler as he tumbles down the stairs.

"Brian!?!" wails Mrs. Thomas, rushing to her son's side. The young man lying on the floor is out cold. Mrs. Thomas looks at him with pure terror in her eyes. Then she stands up, and with cold eyes, she looks up at Diane at the top of the staircase.

"You hurt my son!" Mrs. Thomas shrieks. She pulls out a knife and starts climbing the steps towards Diane.

Diane feels frozen in time. If she were able to think rationally, she would run into her bedroom, lock the door and call the police. But her brain and her feet simply lock in place.

Suddenly a man bursts through the front door. It's Mr. Burke, Diane's neighbour. He's holding the spare key to Diane's cottage that she had once given him. "Mrs. Dimbleby, are you all right?" he yells. "I heard the commotion and thought I better not chance it. You might have been in trouble."

Mr. Burke suddenly sees that she *is* in trouble – a strange woman with what looks to be a very sharp knife is going after Diane. He lunges forward and grabs Mrs. Thomas from behind. Surprisingly, she is able to resist Mr. Burke's strength for a time, but he successfully grapples with Mrs. Thomas to take the knife away from her. Meanwhile, Rufus is standing next to Brian, ready should the man regain consciousness. Diane immediately calls Inspector Crothers.

"Darrell, you were right about Mrs. Thomas and her accomplice. Come quickly! They're both here."

By eleven o'clock Monday night, Mrs. Thomas and her son are both in lock-up at the Shrewsbury Police Station. They have been charged with murder. When Darrell had questioned Brian, he confessed quite easily, taking equal responsibility for the murder of his mother's cousin. The planning had been extensive, he said, starting with him getting hired with Carys. He had never met his mother's cousin, so it had been easy for him to hide his true identity.

Brian said he wanted to help his mom live her last years worry-free. Since she was sure to be the beneficiary of Carys' inheritance, being her closest blood relative, his mum could live the rest of her life in comfort if her cousin was, quite frankly, dead.

Before going home for the night, Darrell heads down to the cells. He's just found out about Carys Jones' will and, out of pure courtesy of course, he decides to share the news with Mrs. Thomas.

Mother and son are in adjoining cells. Mrs. Thomas is sitting on her bunk cursing under her breath. Brian, holding his aching head in one hand, is stretching his arm through the bars in an attempt to console her.

"Well Mrs. Thomas, I finally found out about your cousin's will. You were right – she has one."

"Oh?" says Mrs. Thomas with delusional optimism, not considering the fact that being charged with murder might make any chance of an inheritance impossible.

"She was a generous woman, Carys Jones," says Darrell. "She's left everything to the homeless charity in Shrewsbury."

"What?!?" shrieks Mrs. Thomas. "Surely not the diamond ring though…"

"Oh, you knew about the diamond, did you?" questions Darrell. "In her will, she's requested that it be auctioned off and that the proceeds be donated to the same charity."

Darrell walks away wearing a satisfied smile. *Now that's justice*, he thinks, over the sound of Mrs. Thomas' bellows.

The next day, Darrell pays a special visit to Diane to inform her that she has also been included in Carys' will.

"She's left Rufus to your care," the inspector tells her.

"Well, I was hoping I could keep this 'demanding' companion," she laughs. "He keeps me active and on my toes. And besides, now I don't feel like I'm talking to myself anymore!"

Diane asks if the inspector would like to join them for a walk. Darrell says he would like to, but next time. He hadn't spent any time with his family over the weekend, so he needs to make up for it starting now!

Rufus and Diane find themselves on that same wooded path through the green.

"That's a great idea, Rufus. Let's visit our friend Albert!"

This time, Diane feels no sense of panic. She detaches Rufus from his leash so he can explore all of the natural nooks and crannies off the trail.

Upon arriving at Albert's, she can see him standing over his desk with none other than Richard Butler beside him. Diane knocks on the door.

"Diane, it's so good to see you. Come through, and Rufus too. You know Richard…"

"Yes, of course, hello Richard," Diane says warmly.

"It turns out Richard is interested in history too," says an excited Albert. "He's going to help me with my newspaper archives project."

Albert, Richard, and Diane spend the rest of the afternoon discussing some of the most intriguing newspaper headlines to come out of Shropshire over the last few centuries. As the afternoon transitions into the evening, the three share a small glass of sherry in honour of their friend Carys, knowing all too well that her life was more important than the newspaper headline that described her tragic death.

The End of Murder in the Neighbourhood

Murder on a Yacht

Chapter 1

Apple Mews would normally be characterized by any outsider as quiet, like a strictly-guarded library. And for those outsiders who pass through on a scenic Sunday drive, their minds might, for a fleeting moment, yearn for such a peaceful life. Mind you, these passing whimsies are probably made without the knowledge that Apple Mews has in fact been associated with more than one murder.

But besides that point, it is fairly safe to conclude that all who call it home are happy they live in the Shropshire village.

Still, although Apple Mews only has a couple hundred households, the serene semblance can be quite deceiving. For when you meet the villagers, you'll soon learn that many have boisterous quirks or behaviours, loud both in terms of volume and eccentricity.

At this very moment, in fact, some of Apple Mews' primary school students are up to their regular pranks. Three boys, aged 10 and 11, are kneeling on Mrs. Oakley's front walkway. The focus of their attention are the bottles just delivered by the milkman. The ringleader of the pranksters, Tommy Turner, pulls out a small bottle of blue food colouring. Snickering, while being egged on by his mates, he removes the cap from one of the milk bottles. Less than a second before young Tommy squeezes a drop of blue into the milk, he is stopped by a—

"HALT!"

Tommy drops the food colouring – on the ground, not in the bottle of milk – and looks around.

"Did you hear something?" he asks his mates.

His accomplices nod their heads and shrug their shoulders at the same time. It definitely sounded like a grownup lady's voice, but the only people they see are younger pupils running in the opposite direction up the road.

Tommy picks up the food colouring from the ground.

"HALT!" Diane Dimbleby yells once again, and immediately ducks for cover below her windowsill. She bites her finger to contain her laughter. Staying hidden, she shouts even louder to ensure she's still heard, "You will immediately replace the milk cap, run home as fast as you can and return the blue food colouring to your mother!"

Tommy's accomplices move their heads in every direction, searching for the source of the commanding voice. Tommy, stunned, does not move a muscle.

Diane slowly raises her eyes above the windowsill, and yells "MOVE!"

The boys do not need another warning. Tommy quickly replaces the milk cap, stands and sprints away, even faster than his mates, without looking back.

Once all the boys are out of sight, Diane finally allows herself to release the stream of laughter she had barely contained.

"I've still got it!" she says amusingly to herself, referring to her former years teaching at the same school these boys now attend. Her specialty had been dealing with the eldest, most rambunctious pupils – truth be told she got a kick out of their mischief, although she would never reveal this to her classes.

Diane had taught at Apple Mews' up until a few years ago. Now in her sixties and retired, she is still working, but in another field. Perhaps it was an odd concept some years ago, but for Diane, it had been her plan all along. While teaching had been a passion, she still had to bow to the exigencies of school administrators, parents, and curriculum outcomes. Now, however, she is free to work at her own pace and with creative liberty, doing what she loves best: writing and editing books.

Diane walks next door, collects the milk bottles and walks up to Mrs. Oakley's front door. Immediately after Diane knocks, Mrs. Oakley comes out to the porch.

"I wouldn't have much minded drinking blue milk, but I'm very grateful that you intervened," Mrs. Oakley smiles.

"Ah, you're a good sport Mrs. Oakley!" Diane giggles.

"Won't you come in for a cuppa?"

"I thank you kindly, but I really must finish getting ready for my weekend getaway. Are you sure you don't mind taking care of Rufus in my absence?"

"Not at all my dear! He's good company," Mrs. Oakley responds. "He'll protect me and my milk!"

Diane thanks her neighbour and returns home to finish packing for her trip. Her long-time friend, Mike Davies, has invited her to spend the weekend on the Island of Lundy, which is off the North Devon coast. Lundy is a beautiful isle with a rich and long history, but it is endowed with a variety of reputations.

Some say that it's a drunkard's paradise – the after-hour parties, organized by the thrill seekers who visit the island for scuba diving and climbing excursions, are rumoured to get quite rowdy. On the other hand, some describe Lundy as the most peaceful place on Earth – a haven for birdwatching, serene walks and waking up to the sunrise, not the alarm clock. Still others say it's the perfect place for writers and artists to find inspiration.

Diane, who has visited her friend Mike and Lundy at least three or four times, has not yet decided how she would describe the island. Each time she goes though, it is a welcome change from the hullabaloo that even the small village of Apple Mews seems to generate. On every visit, she makes sure to walk along the beach and enjoy a delicious seafood meal at the island's tavern.

Her friend Mike owns an impressive forty-foot yacht which, during the summer and autumn months, he docks as much as he can at the Lundy Island pier. Each time he invites Diane for a visit, he welcomes her to stay aboard his yacht too.

In recent years, however, Diane's sea legs have become wobblier and she does not enjoy sailing like she used to. She prefers to stay on *terra-firma* as much as possible, or at least while she sleeps. She had proposed a compromise: "I will join you as you sail around the Bristol Channel on Saturday and Sunday, but this time I will spend the night at the Puffin's Nest," she had told him. She has booked the B&B's especially cosy loft bedroom for this trip.

Diane had assured herself that she could handle the daytime on the boat. Their conversations – which never go dry because of their long-time friendship and mutual admiration for reading and writing – would distract her if the waves got too choppy.

Mike of course agreed to the suggested compromise, because he knew that would be the only way that his dear friend would agree to come visit.

Mike is not quite a hermit, but is on the cusp of becoming one. Since retiring from the MI6 – for those not familiar with the world of undercover operations, MI6 is the common name for Britain's Secret Intelligence Service – the 63-year-old native Londoner has taken refuge on his yacht. He likes to keep to himself. In fact, wherever he travels, he's more likely to stay the night on his boat rather than in a hotel.

Those who don't know Mike Davies well would call him shy or aloof. One might conclude that a former MI6 spy has to be that way, living a secretive life and all. *"…the secrecy of our operations and the identity of those who work with us is our foremost principle…"* Perhaps not being able to talk about past covert operations – even traumas – makes getting close to anyone increasingly difficult.

Of course, many readers have had a chance to gain a slight glimpse of insight into the life of Mike Davies. The published author's novels, although works of fiction, are inspired by his intelligence days and even describe some factual events.

And those lucky enough to be a friend of Mike's know that he is as loyal as they come. Diane is one of these lucky few and knows that if she were ever in a pickle, she could turn to him for help. Yet it seems that this time, it is Mike that may need help.

Earlier this Saturday morning, before, as they say, the rooster crowed, Diane drove to Ifracombe as the crow flies. Now crossing the Bristol Channel, aboard the ferry to Lundy Island, she thinks of the conversation she'd had with Mike when he asked her to come for the weekend. She remembers thinking the invitation seemed almost desperate. It was not what he said, but the simplicity of the words he used: it was an earnest request – "Please come." Diane has the sense they will be discussing more than just his latest spy novel.

As the ferry nears Lundy Island's dock, Diane can easily make out the familiar, ghost-white, full head of hair atop her slightly tall friend. She eagerly waves and Mike reciprocates with a basic yet warm salute.

He walks up to the gangway to personally assist Diane off the boat, even though she is very agile for her age, and regardless of the fact that the gangway is easy to manoeuvre. Still, Diane obligingly takes his hand and even allows him to take her valise.

Both standing on the wharf, Mike quickly takes Diane in his arms and gives her a big hug. Although the two friends have been communicating often lately, it must be a year since Diane has visited the island and her friend.

Mike is pleased to see Diane, who is all smiles. The two go back 60 years and have always been comfortable with one another. Although they grew up in different places – Mike in London and Diane in Apple Mews – their two families were friends and got together often. Diane remembers that when they were little, the two shared a boundless imagination and often concocted such elaborate games, like complex treasure hunts or adventures in fantastical worlds.

Now, 60 years later, they find themselves at a place that could be described as just as magical. Together they walk to the Puffin's Nest B&B, so Diane can check in and drop off her suitcase. As they walk up the trail bisecting the moorland of purple heather, Mike comments on the last week's weather, the birth of a new Lundy pony and the latest artist-in-residence.

"She's working on a collection of paintings that simultaneously reflect the island's ecology above and below water. I'm looking forward to seeing them."

Mike stops and looks off in the distance. He holds his binoculars up to his eyes and nods his head. He removes the strap from around his neck and passes the binoculars to Diane.

"Look over there," he says, pointing. "Some of the island's feral goat population.

Diane focuses the lenses until the furry creatures with their pronounced, slightly curled horns come into focus. She slowly moves her body 360 degrees to scan the rest of the landscape. She marvels at the tall brick lighthouse, and then the climbers scaling a vertical granite cliff above a torrent of crashing waves, and then what just might be a colony of puffins way off in the distance.

Still looking through the binoculars, Diane is nearly toppled over by two children sprinting past. Diane laughs at the excited youngsters, as their parents, following behind, apologize.

"Not to worry," says Diane. "It's so refreshing to see children playing outside instead of trapped indoors with their eyes glued to a screen."

"They must be looking for letterboxes," Mike explains.

Lundy Island has numerous letterboxes scattered about. With a map in hand, those up for the challenge can try to find and collect a stamp from each, while solving riddles along the way.

"It sounds like we would have enjoyed that when we were kids," says Diane.

"Who are you kidding? You'd enjoy that now," chuckles Mike.

Inside the bed & breakfast, they are greeted by what seems to be an explosion of puffin knick-knacks, ornaments and curios. Clocks, figurines, plush toys, pictures, cushions and curtains all boast the black and white and orange colours of the seabird of which the accommodation is named after.

"Hello there Mike!" says a woman who runs out from behind an old-fashioned secretary desk cluttered with a puffin bobbleheads, mugs and postcards. "And you must be Diane Dimbleby! Welcome to the Puffin's Nest!"

The proprietor, a Mrs. Poole, does not even wait for Diane to show any proof of payment, but quickly ushers her upstairs to the loft. As fast as Mrs. Poole ran up the stairs, she runs out of the room and back downstairs.

Diane is immediately happy with her decision to stay at the B&B. The sun shining through the south-facing and ceiling windows invite her into the space that has a bed, a desk and private bathroom. Unlike the main floor – there is not a puffin in sight – several vibrant, potted plants add to the welcoming ambience of the room.

Mrs. Poole returns with a tray of scones and iced tea and urges Diane to make herself at home.

"Oh, there's a terrace!" says Diane excitedly, pointing to the small patio adjoined to her top-level room. "Shall we enjoy our snack outside?"

Diane slides open the screen door and Mike carries their tray outside. They each take a seat on a patio chair, content to be the target of the sun's rays.

"I'm so glad to be in your presence Diane on this beautiful day," says Mike, eyes closed.

"And I am happy to be here," says Diane. "But Mike, you must truly tell me why you invited me on this particular occasion. I have a feeling it's more than just to catch up. We've already been talking so much lately"

Mike does not say anything for several minutes. He stares down at the same children from earlier who are now posing next to a letterbox they have just found. Their mother snaps several pictures.

"I didn't want to say anything on the phone," he says finally. "But something's got me spinning. I needed to tell somebody about it. You were the first person that came to mind. I can trust you."

It is about his latest manuscript, Mike explains. He's received some menacing letters and threatening phone calls.

"Someone does not want my book to be published," he says softly.

"But it hasn't been published yet!" says a surprised Diane.

"But I have sent the pages to the publisher," says Mike.

Diane could understand if he received such attention once the book is on the bookshelves– this happened with many controversial books. But how could the contents of the book be leaked at this stage? Only the small team at the publishing house has read the manuscript. Mike would have sent his draft to them via e-mail as was customary these days, rather than sending a hard copy.

"Except they asked me to print the final version and send it to them by post."

This is most curious, Diane thinks. Is Mike being watched? Could a hacker somehow access the documents on Mike's computer? Has somebody bugged the publishing house? Did some fanatic at the post office even cunningly read Mike's pages?

"Do you think it's serious... the threats, I mean?" asks Diane.

Mike doesn't say a word. If Diane could read his mind, she would know he is wondering if he went too far this time. He's never written a "tell-all" autobiography about his time with the MI6 before, but he does tend to recall details from actual events in his novels. Not only does this make the stories more enticing for his readers, it's also been therapeutic for him – a way for him to process what had been a rollercoaster of a profession.

One of the most troubling moments of his career happened at what had been a celebration for others – a time when families and loved ones and a country was reunited. But something happened then that Mike has never been able to get over. He wrote about it in this latest novel – something that perhaps the British government nor the intelligence agency does not want revealed, not even under the guise of fiction.

"The MI6 is not a temporary employer," Mike whispers. "Once you've served under their flag, they will never let you be free to move on with your life."

"Sorry, did you say something Mike?" Diane asks.

"I said, let's go sailing!"

Chapter 2

Even for someone like Diane who does not feel so carefree aboard a ship anymore, today is the perfect day to be sailing around the Bristol Channel. The waters are relatively calm and have a particularly alluring hue, the winds are just the right intensity to fill the boat's sails, and the sun is shining at the most welcoming blaze.

"It's a perfect day for this, Mike," smiles Diane, tucking a grey lock behind her ear. "Thank you."

"Look over there," Mike says.

He's pointing to a handful of grey seals basking atop the rocks near the shore. Close to them, another seal emerges, only exposing its head above the water. Diane watches for some time to see where the head will pop up next. When she squints she can barely make out its whiskers.

Mike steers the ship away from shore into more open waters and drops anchor, so the two friends can enjoy a picnic of sausage rolls and sandwiches and tarts Mrs. Poole from the Puffin's Nest so generously packed them. Mike contributes two mugs and a bottle of sparkling white to the mix.

"If you don't mind terribly, I'd like you to show me those dreadful letters," says Diane after swallowing a morsel of salmon salad sandwich.

Mike continues looking out at the water as if he did not hear Diane's request. Diane decides she'd better not press the issue and instead stands up to stretch her fingers down to her toes.

After a few minutes, Mike gets up and goes down to his cabin. *Oh dear, I've upset him,* thinks Diane.

But her friend returns carrying some pages, the tri-folded creases clearly worn as if they had been opened and closed, read and re-read many times. When Mike passes the pages to Diane, she realizes she had been expecting them to have words formulated from the proverbial letters cut out of a magazine... and maybe even graphic images suggesting violence is near.

Instead they are simply typed, in all caps, in what looks like Times New Roman, size 12. One of the letters says:

"DEAR MIKE DAVIES, KINDLY WITHDRAW YOUR LATEST MANUSCRIPT OR ELSE YOUR DAYS ARE NUMBERED."

The other says:

"THIS IS YOUR LAST WARNING. CANCEL THE BOOK DEAL BEFORE IT'S TOO LATE FOR YOU."

The use of simple font and the absence of shock-value visuals makes the messages even more compelling, Diane thinks. She does not like what these menacing messages are suggesting. In her first-hand experience, and also writing about criminals, she knows there are some people so deranged and so malevolent that they like to torment and frighten their victims before committing the final, dirty deed. They enjoy delivering mental and emotional torture before going in for the *kill*.

"I can see why you've been concerned, Mike," says Diane quietly. And then with more gusto, she says, "Don't you worry. We're going to figure this all out."

When they return to shore, Diane does not take notice of the tourists walking along the beach or the family of ponies grazing up on the hill or the newlywed couple stamping their booklet at a nearby letterbox. All she can think about, all she can wonder, is if her friend really is in trouble or if some person with a disturbing sense of humour is just playing games. And besides, who aside from she and the people working at the publishing house know about Mike's book? With Big Brother watching and the assorted ways for strangers to spy via physical and virtual means, maybe a good deal more people have read her friend's, the retired MI6 agent, manuscript.

Diane takes out her mobile and stares at its screen.

"Mike, is there a phone I can use? My mobile isn't getting any bars."

"Yes, service is spotty on the island," says Mike. "You can use the phone at the tavern."

"Oh goodie! I was hoping to have a meal there tonight."

They walk the short distance to the tavern, called The Granite, which has a sterling reputation, and not just among Lundy Island residents and regulars. Visitors from Devon County and beyond will often make the trip to The Granite for dinner. And more than one London reviewer has said the island pub serves the best fish and seafood in England – Diane would have to agree.

She and Mike are welcomed by The Granite's landlord, Mr. Wilson, standing behind the bar. He's been chatting with someone sitting on bar stool, a fisherman and regular patron from the other side of the channel.

"Hello Mike! And welcome back, Mrs. Dimbleby!"

"Mr. Wilson, how do you remember every single guest who has ever frequented your tavern? It's uncanny," says Diane.

"Ah, it's not every visitor… just the ones worth remembering," Mr. Wilson winks.

"You sure know how to make a lady feel good," says Diane. "Now before I tuck into one of your nice meals, may I use your telephone briefly?"

"By all means, Mrs. Dimbleby, as long as you're not ringing Australia!"

"No sir, not quite that far," Diane laughs.

Mr. Wilson obligingly places the phone on top of the bar in front of Diane. She feels a heart-warming nostalgia as she stares down at the rotary telephone. She has to take a moment to think of the number she's about to dial. In more recent years, she's more familiar with memorizing the positions of numbers on the keypad rather than the numbers themselves. Once she deciphers the actual digits she'll need to 'spin', Diane dials.

"Detective Darrell Crothers," says the voice on the other end of the line.

"Hello, Darrell… it's—"

"Diane? Hello! We haven't spoken since your friend… Mrs. Jones… I meant to get in touch…"

"And me too… and now it seems I need your help."

Inspector Darrell Crothers of the Shrewsbury Police Station – the station responsible for a significant section of Shropshire, including Apple Mews – is a close friend of Diane's. The paths of the retired school teacher and the detective, now in his late 30s, have crossed on several occasions. All of these occasions have had one thing in common – murder. And although at times it causes Darrell to feel great anxiety, Diane normally finds a way to be of great assistance in solving said murders. It's no wonder that she's got a knack for writing murder mysteries. On this occasion however, Diane is asking for Darrell's assistance instead of offering it.

Diane turns her back to Mr. Wilson and the fisherman at the bar so they cannot hear, and tells the inspector all about her friend Mike Davies and the threatening letters and calls he's been receiving because of his manuscript. Diane knows that Darrell has the resources and know-how to assist in this investigation… before it's too late.

"Well, you caught me right before I was going on a two-day fishing holiday," says Darrell. "I suppose if your friend Mike is willing to take me sailing I would be willing to change my plans and come to Lundy to take a look at those letters."

"Oh thank you, Darrell! Thank you most kindly!"

Diane turns around and gives Mike a thumbs up. Mike lifts his shoulders, confused. He's unsure of who Diane is even talking to.

After Diane hangs up the phone, she and Mike sit down at a table near a window with an ample view of the sea. The wooden table is bare of any decorative pieces which is just fine, as the quality of cuisine – prepared by Mr. Wilson's wife and son – and the people who visit the tavern are more than enough to make the atmosphere most pleasing.

"I called my friend, Inspector Darrell Crothers…to help," explains Diane.

"But, I'm not sure Diane if we should involve anybody at this point," Mike, slightly protests. "Can we trust him?"

"Don't you worry, Mike. He's got a good head on his shoulders, this one."

Mr. Wilson takes Mike and Diane's dinner orders after serving them a couple pints of local brew. As they wait for their meals, more people trickle in to the tavern. A man, whose grey hair is mostly covered by his beige Tilley hat, is now sitting at the bar next to the fisherman. Diane recognizes him from at least one past visit.

"Who is that?" whispers Diane.

"Oh that's Shaun Boyle, the island's head marine conservationist," says Mike. "Nice chap."

Mr. Boyle's striking Irish accent makes it hard for anyone within earshot to resist eavesdropping.

"I dunnoooo," says Shaun Boyle. "I think that may be a wee bit premature. Ammmm… a sheriff on Lundy Island?"

The fisherman says something in response to the conservationist. Diane and Mike subconsciously lean towards him attempting to hear what the fisherman is saying but his utterances are much too soft.

"Sure we sometimes get some eejits here that drink too much and get langers and make some noise," continues Mr. Boyle, "but most people that come over are not dodgy… most people respect the land and the people and the good work we're doing here… we don't need a sheriff I don't think."

Before Diane can ask Mike his opinion on the merits of law enforcement on Lundy Island, their food arrives. Diane's mouth waters at the sight of her beer-battered fish and chips and mushy peas and at Mike's unique sample plate of whelks, crab, sausage, cheese and bread – something not advertised on the menu but mutually concocted by Mike and the chef.

They enjoy their meal thoroughly and neither Diane or Mike are disappointed, even though there is always the chance of disappointment when a restaurant becomes a favourite and expectations are built up so high.

"Lundy Island is truly a special place, isn't it Mike?" says Diane, wiping her mouth after the last bite.

Mike answers with a completely honest smile. This evening together in the tavern goes back to simpler times and allows the two to forget about any worries, from the past or present. They even join in a game of bridge with a pair of locals, even though Mike would normally avoid such interactions with acquaintances. But Diane's social manner is a good influence on the secluded man. The first time he and Diane take their tricks, the retired ops man even finds that he has been enjoying himself.

After finishing their pints and playing who knows how many games of cards, Diane reveals a yawn. It's 11 o'clock and she's not sure if the Puffin's Nest has a curfew. She certainly does not want to disturb Mrs. Poole if she's sleeping.

"I think it's best I turn in for the night," Diane says, disappointed to leave the fun.

"I better be going too," Mike says.

They thank their new friends for the card game and say goodnight to Mr. Wilson, who is still standing behind the bar.

As Mike walks Diane back to the Puffin's Nest, they talk about happy things, like funny shared moments when their families caravanned together, and they ask each other about favourite things, like puddings, films and holidays. They do not talk once about threatening letters, and Diane does not even feel she needs to remind Mike that Inspector Darrell Crothers is arriving on the ferry the next morning. They've already arranged that they'll both be at the pier to welcome the inspector.

After seeing that Diane is safely tucked inside the bed and breakfast, Mike walks back to his yacht with a spring in his step. He decides that tomorrow he'll take his friend sailing to a spot he's never taken her before but thinks she'll adore. It's an area of sea caves and he hopes he'll be able to convince her to snorkel around them. *She's still very adventurous*, he thinks.

Nothing can dissuade Mike's good mood, that is until he tucks into his own bed on the yacht. It's when his eyes shut that his mind starts to wander.

His reverie gradually remembers the sounds of hammers and chisels against concrete, the cheers of people dancing in the streets to pop music being played at full blast...

Although back then, he was never 'off the clock', Mike saw no reason why he could not celebrate too. It was a happy time for he and his team as well. Mike let down his guard and even allowed himself to bop up and down to the music. He remembers looking down to see two children facing one another, and twirling in circles while holding hands.

Mike remembers staring out across the happy crowd, thinking *this is history in the making*. And then a loud *BANG!* pierced through the soundscape.

The next morning, Diane is awoken from a sound sleep by the call of a puffin-themed cuckoo clock downstairs. It is just as well because in an hour, Inspector Darrell Crothers should be arriving on the ferry.

Mrs. Poole must be reading Diane's mind, or listening for any sign of movement from her room, because as soon as Diane turns on the tap to splash water on her face she hears a knock.

"Breakfast, Mrs. Dimbleby," pipes Mrs. Poole from the other side of the bedroom door.

Diane, still wiping the sleep from her eyes, rushes out to answer. She opens the door to see the woman balancing two trays, one in each hand. One has fresh-baked scones, a selection of jams, and a fruit bowl on. The other is holding a teapot, teacup and a small carafe of milk.

"I could have come down to get my breakfast," says Diane. "How did you climb the stairs with both those trays? How long have you been awake?"

Mrs. Poole simply laughs, sets the trays down on top of the desk inside the room and scurries back down the stairs.

"Ta, Mrs. Poole," Diane calls after her.

Instead of resuming her 'bird bath', Diane digs into one of the cinnamon scones – while they are still warm – and decides on a blueberry jelly as a complement. She takes a few moments to linger over her hot cup of tea and breakfast, and then returns to the bathroom to get ready for the day.

Downstairs, Mrs. Poole pops out from behind her desk to bid Diane a delightful day. After a little startled jump, Diane wishes Mrs. Poole the same, and goes outside to walk down to the dock.

Diane looks at her watch and realizes there's still 20 minutes before the ferry is due. She slows her pace down to a meander and notices that the bright blue sky is devoid of any clouds. Another gorgeous day – she's been lucky this trip.

For the first time taking this path between the Puffin's Nest and the boat dock, Diane notices what must be one of the letterboxes Mike was telling her about.

I really should try to complete this letterbox trail some time, thinks Diane.

Diane walks up to the letterbox and opens it. Inside she finds a stamp and ink pad. She picks up the stamp and turns it over. When she sees the imprint's shape, she lets out a gasp.

"It's just ink," she says after a moment, to reassure herself.

Ink the colour of blood red is partially covering the stamp; it's shaped like a black crow in flight.

Laughing her silly reaction off, Diane continues down to the wharf. She finds herself on the pier, alone. Mike had told her he would meet her here, but perhaps he is still sleeping. *He is still sleeping.* She decides not to go wake him up. There's no need for them both to welcome Darrell, plus she does not want to miss the inspector's arrival which is due to happen any minute.

It's funny how just the other day, Diane saw Mike waiting for her on the pier… and now she is waving to Darrell coming in on the ferry.

"God bless him," Diane whispers out loud. "He's already good at what he does and he's still got many years to go."

When the ferry is docked, the inspector waits for a family of six (all wearing matching striped shirts) and a couple (who by all accounts appear to be on their honeymoon) to disembark, before joining Diane on the pier. He holds out his hand to shake Diane's, but she ignores the gesture and wraps her arms around his back. She's grown fond of the inspector after the time they've spent 'working cases together'.

"So Mike was going to meet us here too, but he's still asleep," says Diane. "We had a late night last night… well, late for us old fogies… not for you I'm sure!"

"Well, before we go see him, is there anything else you should tell me?" Darrell asks.

While walking the detective towards the marina, Diane repeats the information about the threatening letters and phone calls that Mike has received. She also tells him that the book, although fiction, might make some people in power angry. Finally she tells him that a hard copy of the manuscript has been sent to the publishing house.

Before she can tell the inspector anything further they have arrived at the small port where a half dozen sailboats and a few fishing boats are moored.

"That's his," says Diane, pointing to the tallest, and what appears to be the newest, sailboat of the lot. "That's strange," she adds.

"What's strange?" asks Darrell as they approach Mike's boat.

"All of the hatches are closed… and the windows too."

Diane tells Crothers that it's highly unusual for Mike to shut everything up like that. Normally he leaves at least one or two cabin windows open. He loves the smell of the sea and would feel cooped up otherwise.

"Maybe it was chilly last night," Darrell suggests.

"Or maybe he's taking more precautions," Diane whispers, her voice trailing. What she's thinking is maybe Mike was afraid to have an intruder catch him unawares.

Standing on the jetty in front of Mike's yacht, Diane calls his name. With no answer she calls again, this time louder.

"Maybe he's gone to the…" Diane's voice trails again. There aren't very many places to go to run errands on Lundy Island. Still, it wouldn't be impossible for Mike to forget to meet her and go to The Granite for some breakfast.

Diane climbs aboard with Darrell following behind her. Nothing seems amiss. Mike keeps a clean ship. Diane calls his name again.

Darrell walks around to the cabin entrance and awkwardly knocks on the hatch. Receiving no answer, he opens the hatch door and slowly goes down the steps. With not much sunlight accessing the space, Darrell feels for his torch attached to his belt. He turns it on and shines it slowly around the cabin.

He suddenly stops scanning and zeroes in on a particular spot. He gradually steps towards the focus of his attention, shining the torch resolutely.

"Is there room for me to come down?" asks Diane.

"No! Stay there!" yells Darrell uncharacteristically. "And don't touch anything!"

"Well I say," says a bewildered Diane.

Darrell stops when he's almost touching the edge of the cabin bed. He's never met him, but can only assume that this is Mike Davies lying here. From a distance, one might surmise that this man is sound asleep in his bed, save for one particular detail. And that particular detail is that it appears, at first glance, that his head has been gruesomely bashed in.

With no sign of a snore or a breath, the inspector can only conclude that Mike Davies is not sound asleep, but dead.

Chapter 3

Sergeant Sean Golden can hardly believe it. He prefers to stay standing, and paces back and forth on the ferry as he rides over to Lundy Island. In his years stationed at the Barnstaple police office he's never once been called over to the island for a homicide. He's had to pursue disorderly conduct from drunks and drug abusers, sure, but never a homicide.

Even in the entire County of Devon the murder and homicide rate is low – 15 tops a year – and in North Devon where he is based, there is generally next to none.

And to think, he had been feeling really good about the security of his county. The Devon police force had just organized another successful Firearms Amnesty event. Of course, most of the people who handed in guns were probably not the sort of people that would kill or maim, but turning in their rifles, shotguns and other arms helps prevent any possibility of them falling into the wrong hands.

The 200 arms turned in across Devon would be scrap metal by now transformed into unrecognizable, unthreatening pieces.

Even some handguns were turned in; not just antique revolvers or pistols from avid historians and collectors, but actual, modern-day handguns. (After the atrocious massacre when Thomas Hamilton murdered 16 children at a primary school in Dunblane, Scotland, the British Parliament effectively banned the possession of handguns.)

That is the beauty of such an amnesty event – no questions asked – so people could hand in banned weapons without fear of repercussion. Sergeant Sean Golden had been honoured to play a part in the initiative of reducing the number of firearms in the County. About 20 guns had been turned into the Barnstaple station – mostly hunting rifles and a BB gun – but this also reassured him that he was living in one of the safest areas of the country… even the world.

Sergeant Golden doesn't know if this particular homicide he's been called to happened from a gunshot or another means. All he was told over the phone – *by an Inspector Crothers, was it?* – was that a homicide happened and the body was at the marina. Perhaps it had not been done on purpose. Maybe a party got out of hand and items were thrown or people were pushed or who knows what…

Sergeant Golden begins to shake ever so slightly. Being 195 cm tall and muscular from his neck down to his ankles – he works out on the weights and a bike he set up right behind his desk at the Barnstaple station – many imagine him to be an insensitive bloke. Yet truth be told, the smallest form of violence, against person or property, touches the heart Golden wears on his sleeve.

The sergeant takes in a deep breath and reminds himself that he's the Island's primary law enforcement contact. He's been called, and he is responding.

Diane can hardly believe this has happened. She had not actually believed there was anything really profound to worry about. She had asked Darrell to come to the island only as a precaution - she did not truly think Mike's life was in danger. But now Mike Davies, her lifelong friend, is dead.

"Diane!" Darrell says, a little louder than he'd like. Sitting next to her, he had said her names several times without her responding. Diane is breathing rather quickly, too quickly, and he needs to calm her down before she turns blue.

Diane finally looks up at the inspector who is holding her hand and staring at her with concerned eyes.

"I... I... I think I need to go home, Darrell... can you take me home now?" Diane says.

Darrell does not say anything for some time. He simply puts his arm around her and lets her cry muffled sobs into his chest. They sit there, on the edge of the pier next to Mike's yacht, for several minutes.

Once Diane's sobs subside, Darrell says, "I can walk you back to the Puffin's Nest for a rest if you want. I should stay here at least until the sergeant from the mainland arrives."

"Oh, you should stay for the entire investigation!" says Diane, suddenly snapping out of her state of despair.

"Maybe once you've had a wee bit of a rest, you can help by doing what you do best – using that brain of yours."

"Darrell, we must stay right here – we need to figure out who has killed Mike!" Diane says adamantly, as if it had been Darrell and not her who, just minutes ago, had suggested they leave the island.

Darrell hadn't let Diane go down into the cabin to see the body of her friend, but he had told her that Mike had left this world and not by natural causes.

Diane face becomes resolute, like she's now ready to play the role of investigator rather than grieving chum. Before she stands up to make her way onto the yacht again, Sergeant Sean Golden approaches.

"Inspector Darrell Crothers?" he asks quietly.

"Yes, you must be Sergeant Sean Golden. Thank you for coming so quickly," Darrell says, shaking the Devon County police officer's hand.

The local sergeant is at least a head taller than Darrell and towers over Diane, and yet his height does not give him any edge in the confidence department. Both Darrell and Diane are seasoned when it comes to solving homicides; this would be Sergeant Golden's second homicide case, and the first that he's in charge of.

However, what he's lacking in 'major crimes' experience, he more than makes up for in empathy and gentleness. He places a tender hand on Diane's shoulder, telling her he's sorry for her loss.

"Inspector Crothers told me the victim was a friend of yours," Golden says.

Diane nods and gives the sergeant an appreciative smile.

"Come, Sergeant Golden. I'll take you down to the scene," says Darrell. "Diane, will you be okay waiting here?"

"I'll head back to the Puffin's Nest," says Diane. "Not to sleep but to start working. You can find me there."

Golden tentatively follows Darrell onto the yacht and down the stairs into the cabin. Although he has been expecting to see the corpse, the dead body of Mike Davies still catches him off guard. The amount of blood and the part of his now deformed head nearly makes the sergeant physically ill.

"That's not a gunshot, is it?" asks Golden timidly.

"No. It needs to be confirmed by a medical professional, but it appears to be a blow from an extremely heavy object," says Darrell. "And since an object like that is not close to the body, it's pretty certain it's not an accident."

"Oh, I see… and the body doesn't smell, does it? I thought it would smell, surely, being dead and all," says Golden.

"No, he hasn't been dead long enough," Darrell explains patiently.

"And would this be murder or manslaughter… and if it's manslaughter, would it be involuntary or voluntary…. and if it's involuntary would it be… oh, I'm sorry Inspector Crothers. Of course, we can't know any of that until we find out who's responsible… I'm just a wee bit nervous, that's all."

Darrell tells the sergeant to relax and assures him that he was the same way on his first few murder cases. Darrell tells him that, if he does not mind of course, he would like to handle the case. After all, Mrs. Diane

Dimbleby is a close friend of his and the murder victim is a close friend of hers, and since he discovered the body, he has the benefit of probably being the first on the scene since the dirty act was committed. Of course, he would run it by both Golden's superintendent and his own to make sure he has their permission.

"I'd like to see the case through to the end," says Darrell, "but only if you don't mind."

"That's brilliant," says a relieved Golden; then, trying not to sound too excited, he says, "No, I don't mind. I have some other work I should be getting on with anyway."

Darrell smiles. Some police officers can be very possessive of their jurisdiction, but it seems like Golden is most agreeable to share. In fact, he's keen to get out of the immediate vicinity of Mike Davies' body, and does so at a speed much faster than you would expect from such a towering figure.

"Oh, Sergeant Golden," says Darrell, calling after the policeman. "Hold up."

Darrell walks up the steps to the deck of the yacht to see Golden already halfway down the pier. "Golden!" he calls again, which has the intended effect this time.

The sergeant slowly turns around, worried the inspector has changed his mind about taking charge of the case. Heading down, he slowly walks back from whence he came.

"Golden, before you go, can I just ask a favour?" asks Darrell.

"Oh certainly, certainly, please excuse me… I don't know what's gotten into me," says the sergeant.

"Understood," says Darrell. "Can you tell me where the closest GP might be? I need him or her to come and examine the body."

"GP, sir?"

"General practitioner… a doctor… just until I can get my medical examiner, Dr. Jackson, down here. I'll call him at once, but it will still take several hours for him to arrive."

The sergeant tells Darrell that there's actually a retired doctor living on Lundy Island, a Dr. Cartwright. Before Golden goes to fetch him, he lends Darrell his satellite phone – a device he brings with him to the island due to the unreliable mobile service – so the inspector can call Dr. Jackson.

"I knew you had some brain to go along with your brawn," Darrell says with a wink.

Over the phone, Dr. Jackson is not quick to agree to make the lengthy trip to Devon County. After the inspector manages to negotiate adequate compensation – they decided that Darrell would bring the medical examiner a packed lunch every day for a month, and not just a simple sandwich mind you, but a packed lunch that could be described as 'gourmet' – Dr. Jackson agrees to make the trip to Barnstaple to examine the body of Mike Davies formally.

After Darrell resists the temptation to call his wife and children to say, *"I'm calling you on a satellite phone… that means we're being connected by satellites orbiting around space,"* he sees Sergeant Golden running back towards the marina. An older gentleman, Dr. Cartwright, is hurrying to keep up behind him.

By the looks of some leftover shaving cream on Dr. Cartwright's cheeks, one can surmise that Golden did not give the retired physician much time to ponder the request to come and examine the deceased.

The doctor does not seem to mind. As soon as he introduces himself to Darrell he immediately gets to work. At the top of the yacht's cabin stairs, he asks Golden to hand him his leather Gladstone bag.

"Shall I call about a forensics team, Sir?" Golden asks the inspector.

"Yes, thank you Golden," Darrell says. "I think you're much more suited for this line of inquiry than you think."

As it may be a long wait before forensics can arrive, Darrell joins the doctor in the cabin and takes numerous pictures, using his phone, while Mike Davies is still *in situ*.

The contents of the space reinforce its status as a permanent residence. Photos – some of far-off, tropical places, some of more familiar places, like the Frankfurt Opera House, perhaps – hang on the cabin walls. A stack of books balances next to a lamp on a side table standing next to the bed. A short closet is jam-packed with shirts and trousers hanging from plastic hangers in sporadic order.

Whoever did this knew that Mike essentially lived on this yacht.

"So doctor, can you confirm cause of death?" Darrell asks as Dr. Cartwright replaces his instruments inside his bag.

"Yes, as you suspected, cause of death is most probably a severe blow to the head. This is not my area of expertise, but if I had to wager a reliable guess, I would say he died in the early hours of the morning. I'll note his body temperature for the medical examiner."

"Good, Golden can relay this information to Dr. Jackson when he takes the body to the morgue in Barnstaple," says Darrell. "Thank you Dr. Cartwright for making yourself available at short notice."

Darrell and Dr. Cartwright emerge out of the cabin to see Golden with a slumped posture and looking rather pale... again.

"Are you quite alright?" Dr. Cartwright asks the sergeant, reaching up to feel his forehead.

"I heard the inspector say... you'd like me to accompany the body to the morgue, sir?"

"Why yes, Golden. Now don't you fret. I meant what I said. You have a knack for investigations... detective work. You just need the experience."

Golden's colour returns and he smiles. "I don't have a cadaver pouch, but I bet I could track down a non-porous material quickly – a tarpaulin perhaps – to transport the corpse."

"A non-porous material you say! Well, who's the smart one now?" Darrell cheers. "Might be best to ask one of your mates on the island to help you carry the body over to the mainland... and keep it low profile... you don't want to spook any tourists on the ferry."

"Right!" Golden says, determined.

Golden sets off to locate a non-porous material and someone that has the stomach to help him move a dead body – truth be told, most of the island's residents could probably endure such a deed. Dr. Cartwright volunteers to stay with Mike Davies until the sergeant returns, so Darrell can go and check on Diane at the Puffin's Nest.

After the short climb up the moorland, Mrs. Poole greets the inspector at the bed and breakfast's front door. It's been some time since a male as young and dashing as Darrell Crothers has visited the Puffin's Nest.

"Come through, come through," says Mrs. Poole, a little too keenly. "You must be lost. Come sit and have a cup of tea while we figure out where you're trying to go."

Darrell chuckles. "If this is the Puffin's Nest, I'm exactly where I need to be."

"Oh my," blushes the bed and breakfast's proprietor.

"I'm here to see one of your guests... Mrs. Diane Dimbleby."

Mrs. Poole, slightly disappointed, but remaining as pleasant as always, brings Darrell to Diane's room. She takes the liberty of knocking for the inspector.

"Yes?" Diane says, sounding distracted.

"You have a visitor... a young man... who says he knows you."

"Oh yes, indeed… you can come in Darrell!"

When Darrell opens the door, he sees Diane sitting at her desk intently bent over her laptop. She has been hard at work meticulously reading Mike Davies' manuscript, and not for the first time. In addition to the staff at the publishing house, Diane has also read Mike's novel before. A while back he sent her a digital copy which has been saved on her computer since. She is in the middle of reading one of the more 'hair-raising' passages – one dealing with an intricate strategy used by the MI6 some time ago to extract a fellow agent from an unfriendly territory – when Darrell arrives.

"Do you know much about the Berlin Wall, Darrell?" Diane asks, looking up from her laptop.

"Of course I know there was a wall that divided Germany, but I can't say I know much… why?"

"Well, you would have just been a child or barely a teenager when the Wall came down," says Diane.

Darrell takes a seat, sensing the retired teacher is about to give him a history lesson. He's happy to take a rest for a few minutes. Plus Diane does not normally prattle on, so when she has a lot to say, she normally has an important point to make.

Diane asks Darrell to imagine waking up to find out that a barrier had been created right in the middle of his city – a barrier that nobody is allowed to cross. That means if his friends or relatives or job or favourite place to visit are on the other side, he is not permitted to go to or visit them.

This happened in Berlin, Diane continues. On August 12, 1961, at midnight, East German soldiers and police were commanded to close the border, which crossed through Berlin and divided East and West Germany. Literally neighbours, families and friends were separated. Students could not reach their university to continue their studies. East Germans who had loved ones in a hospital in West Berlin could not go and visit them.

At first the wall was made of barbed wire and blocks, and then it became more fortified and made of cement. Some people successfully snuck over the wall, but others were captured or killed. Diane tells Darrell that one of Mike's colleagues, another British agent, had been trapped in East Berlin, but he did not try to escape while the wall stood.

In 1989, protestors convened next to the Wall which urged the East German government to reopen the border between the East and the West. The gates along the wall were opened. This was the beginning of the fall of the Berlin Wall.

"It was a major celebration – you might remember seeing some of the news coverage on the tele," says

Diane. "But something went dreadfully wrong with Mike's colleague."

"So Mike was an MI6 agent?" asks an astonished Darrell

"Yes, and some of his actual experiences with the MI6 are featured in his latest manuscript," Diane explains. "Even though it's a work of fiction, I fear that what he's revealed may have provoked someone to shut him up."

Diane gives the inspector a thumb drive that has a copy of the manuscript on it. She tells Darrell that he should read it as its contents may be essential for solving her friend's murder. That is, if the story is in fact the killer's motive.

Diane also tells Darrell that other than herself, the only people that she knows of who have seen the manuscript are the staff at the publishing house. But with all the latest talk of hacking and spying, one could never be sure how many eyes are lurking about.

"How did you read the manuscript so quickly, Diane? You haven't even been in your room here for an hour. And did you take this thumb drive from the cabin this morning? You know that you shouldn't be taking anything from a crime scene..."

"I've been reading Mike's pages since he began writing the novel," says Diane. "With the publishers' permission, Mike asked me to be his editor on this project. I agreed."

Darrell stares at her blankly for an instant. Then he stands up quickly, practically pouncing towards the closet. He opens it and finds what he's after – Diane's suitcase. He swings it open and lays it on her bed. Forgetting all his manners, he starts grabbing clothes out of the closet and throwing them in the case.

"Darrell!?! What's gotten into you???" an alarmed Diane asks.

A knock comes at the door. "Everything alright in there?" warbles Mrs. Poole from behind the door.

"Yes!" Diane and Darrell yell at the same time.

Darrell listens for the sound of Mrs. Poole's feet going back down the stairs, and then says, "Diane, don't you see? If the killer murdered Mike because of the book, he or she might know that you are the book's editor. And if they know that, you may be next on their hit list. I do not want you anywhere near this place!"

"But—"

"There is no argument you can make that will subtract from the fact that you might not be safe here. I want you on the very next ferry off this island."

But Diane isn't a former MI6 agent. She isn't privy to British Secret Service operations. And it wasn't her that wrote the passages that allude to actual events that some people in power may not want made public. She has just been correcting some basic grammatical errors, the odd typo, and in a few cases has improved phraseology.

Still, she *does* know what happened 25 years ago at the border between East and West Berlin. It was a particular incident Mike wrote about. He thought he had been safe including it in a book of *fiction*. But perhaps he had been wrong.

Diane wonders though, who's to say he wasn't murdered for some completely different reason, like for the classic motives of greed, heartbreak or revenge?

Chapter 4

After it travels through a hallway of doors labelled 'Motive A' through 'Z', Diane's mind returns to the loft on the top floor of the Puffin's Nest Bed and Breakfast. Her eyes focus back on the suitcase that Darrell continues to fill with her very own clothing, which she finds only slightly disturbing. It'd be as if her son or nephew, if she had either, were packing her clothes, and she's nowhere near the state of needing someone to do her packing.

Before Darrell can open the drawer holding her knickers, Diane says, "You said yourself that I could help by doing what I do best – using my brain to help you with this case."

"That was before I knew you were working as the murder victim's editor," says Darrell. "And like *you* said, the book might be the motive."

"That doesn't mean I'm in danger, surely."

"The killer might still be in the area. Don't you think that if he knows that the editor of Mike Davies' book is on the island, he'll want that editor – you – dead!?!"

"Ok, there's no need to blow a fuse," says Diane, feeling deflated in purpose.

She agrees to leave the island as long as Darrell lets her finish her own packing.

Downstairs, Diane informs Mrs. Poole that she is checking out, but that Inspector Darrell Crothers would take over the loft if she has no objections. The inn owner swings her arms in excitement. She's overjoyed to hear the detective would be staying at none other than the Puffin's Nest.

Diane bends down to pick up the items that Mrs. Poole so boisterously knocked to the floor. She stares down at a letter she's just picked up. It's one that Mrs. Poole had been writing to her sister who lives in County Durham. It isn't so much that the sisters write to one another out of fear that the art of letter writing will become extinct – it's more because neither can stand the other's voice. They much prefer to communicate by post rather than by telephone.

"I'll take that thank you," Mrs. Poole says, swiping the letter from Diane's hands.

"Oh terribly sorry," says Diane. "Thank you, Mrs. Poole, for your hospitality."

Mrs. Poole's letter has stirred up Diane's vault of recent memories. Specifically it has brought her attention to what *had* been an inconspicuous detail, one that the unconscious has collected and has waited for the conscious to catch up. Specifically Diane is remembering the threatening letters that Mike had shown her – the ones that so cruelly addressed him.

When Diane had held the letters in her own hands, while aboard friend's yacht, she must have subconsciously held each of the pages up to the sun. She remembers now seeing a faint image, a watermark. And if it is what she envisions now, the watermark is a familiar one.

She remembers the symbol with wholehearted focus now – a calligraphic *CP*. Diane knows she's seen stationary with that same watermark before, and recently too. The *CP* stands for 'Copse Publishers', the name of the publishing house in Birmingham that Mike has been working with.

The first time Diane read the name, she thought it said 'Corpse Publishers'. Mike naturally corrected her mistake, explaining the name 'Copse' (which means a small wood or thicket of trees) had been chosen to pay tribute to Birmingham's reputation as a city of many trees and parks.

The threatening letters sent to her friend were written on stationary from Copse Publishers. That almost certainly means that someone who works at the publishing house, who has read the manuscript, sent Mike the threats. Did that same person kill him?

Diane stops herself from shouting out what she's just remembered. She shouldn't say such things in front of Mrs. Poole, plus Darrell has enough on his plate right now with supervising the forensic team who will be coming to work the scene on the yacht and coordinating with the Barnstaple morgue to receive Dr. Jackson, so he can conduct the formal autopsy.

At the pier, Diane and Darrell run into Sergeant Golden. He's recruited the conservationist, Shaun Boyle, to help him transport Mike's body to the mainland. The corpse is wrapped in an aqua blue tarp, but ingeniously a long piece of rain gutter is sticking out on either end to make the 'load' resemble some sort of construction material.

Still, as soon as Diane sees the mass wrapped in blue, she knows exactly what, or rather *who*, it is. She becomes weak in the knees and Darrell holds her elbow to keep her from falling. After a couple of long breaths with her eyes closed, Diane regains her composure.

"Inspector Crothers, Mrs. Dimbleby, this is Shaun Doyle," says Sergeant Golden. "He's agreed to help me… you know…."

"This has put the heart crossways in me," says Mr. Doyle. "I just can't believe it. A murder? On Lundy Island!?"

"Shhhhhh!" Diane, Darrell and Sergeant Golden shush simultaneously. Luckily the couple and the single gentleman also waiting for the ferry seem not to have heard.

When the ferry arrives, Darrell gives Diane a hug, something he rarely initiates with his older friend and fellow crime solver. He tells her that he will call her at home to give her an update on how the investigation is going.

Diane follows close behind Sergeant Golden and Mr. Doyle, who manage to carry Mike's body as if they are seasoned construction workers headed to their next job. Diane sits in the row behind them, and several times during the ferry ride finds herself placing her hand on top of the tarp covering her friend's body.

Upon reaching Barnstaple, Diane leaves it up to Sergeant Golden to accompany Mike's corpse to the morgue. She feels relieved to be in the driver's seat of her car again – it seems like it has been ages, even though she's only been away since early yesterday.

The whole drive back to Apple Mews, Diane's mind alternates between thinking about who to notify about her friend's death – as far as she knows, Mike has no living relatives – and Copse Publishers.

In the past, out of all the staff at the publishing house, she's only corresponded with Julie Petrie, the publishing house's executive director, and only by e-mail.

Diane wonders how tight the security is at a publisher's office. It could be possible that someone not even connected to Copse Publishers broke in, read Mike's manuscript and even used some of the publisher's stationary to write the threats. *This would be an intriguing plot line for my next crime novel,* Diane thinks for a brief moment. Her mind quickly shifts to, *how dare I think about my friend's murder in that way right now!*

She suddenly slams on the brakes. The Border Collie in front of her car stops just as quickly. Standing in the middle of the road the dog stares at Diane. If Diane had been lost in thought just a few seconds longer she could have hit the poor dog. The Border Collie stares a moment longer, not with malice in his eyes but concern almost, then finishes crossing the road into an adjacent farmer's field.

"I wish you were here, Rufus!" Diane yells aloud. She is so used to taking her canine companion with her everywhere, but she couldn't have brought him to Lundy Island since sailing was on the books.

Diane continues the drive, more focused this time, and manages to return to Apple Mews without any other mishaps. As soon as she pulls her car into her driveway, she can hear Rufus barking next door. It seems that he is as excited to see her as she him.

Diane runs over to Mrs. Oakley's and knocks, trying not to do so frantically. Mrs. Oakley opens the door, and Rufus bursts out and jumps up to greet his friend and caretaker. Diane wraps her arms around Rufus' shoulders and nuzzles her nose into his fuzzy back.

When she stands up, Diane finally notices the new… 'fur-style' Rufus is donning. The grey terrier's hair that normally hangs naturally over his eyes and nose has been tied into an assortment of buns, each held together with a pink bow.

"Oh my, Rufus, don't you look dashing," Diane giggles.

"I was trying to think of a way to keep his hair clean – it gets in the way when he eats, don't you think?" says Mrs. Oakley. "Perhaps I got a little carried away."

"Nothing wrong with a new style from time to time," Diane laughs again. "Was he a good boy for you while I was away?"

"He was at that, although one time he hid my socks on me, he did! He's a smart one, aren't you Rufus? A little rascal I suspect too."

Mrs. Oakley scratches the terrier behind the ears, sad to see him go. Diane thanks her neighbour for taking care of Rufus and tells her that once she's settled back in, she'll have to invite her over for a nice dinner. What she does not tell Mrs. Oakley is that the invitation may have to wait until the case of Mike Davies' murder is solved.

Diane quickly brings their things inside and then takes Rufus for a walk. Perhaps she is craving the fresh air and exercise as much as or more than the terrier. Diane is feeling spooked to the bone and needs to try and settle her mind.

When their feet touch the village green, Diane unclips the leash, allowing Rufus to run free. Diane follows behind quickly. The power-walker pace is helping her angst morph into calm... that is until, whilst coming around the bend, she smacks into her dear friend Albert.

Diane lets out a squeal, while Albert is more than pleased to see her. Although their relationship is technically platonic, the two retirees are each other's closest companions and confidants. They each envision, in the back of their minds, that they will marry, although the topic has never been broached aloud.

Albert immediately breaks out into a spiel about his latest local history project. "I am not certain… but in or around this very spot, is where the very first recorded game of cricket was played!"

"My stars! The very first game of cricket in the world was right here?!"

"I didn't say that, my dear Diane. But the very first game of cricket in Apple Mews was on this spot... or a spot near this spot."

Diane laughs quite hard until her laughter turns to crying.

"Oh, what is it my dear?" Albert asks, as he passes Diane a handkerchief. "You look like you've seen a ghost."

Albert places an arm around his friend. When Diane catches her breath, she tells him everything: about what's happened to Mike aboard his yacht at Lundy Island, about the threatening letters, about the manuscript and her suspicion that it is the motive.

"You have to promise not to share this with anybody, Albert," Diane says quietly.

"Of course I won't. But what can I do to help?"

"You've already done it," says Diane with a smile. "I feel better having told you. And now I know what I should do next."

Diane wishes Albert luck with his history tour of the game of cricket and reminds him of their upcoming 'mead and mystery' get-together. She whistles for Rufus to come, reattaches his leash, and quickly walks back home.

After filling Rufus' water bowl, Diane turns on her computer and Googles 'Copse Publishers' to look up its phone number. Although it's Sunday afternoon, she's decided to call the executive director anyway. She'll leave a message on Mrs. Petrie's voicemail and that way it will be there waiting for her first thing tomorrow. It's crucial that Diane get a hold of her as soon as possible. And she doesn't want to send the director a message to her work e-mail address, because who knows who will be snooping in the office today.

As she listens to the ringtone, Diane tries to mentally prepare exactly what she'll say on Mrs. Petrie's voicemail. But instead of hearing "You've reached the voicemail of Julie Petrie…," somebody picks up after just two rings.

"Hello, Copse Publishers."

"Um… yes… um… I'd like to speak to Julie Petrie please."

"This is she."

"I didn't expect that you'd be in the office today. I'm sorry if I'm disturbing you. My name is Diane Dimbleby."

"Oh Diane! It's so nice to finally speak to you. I'm such a big fan of your latest book. And you've been doing a smashing job editing Mike's book."

"Mrs. Petrie—"

"Please, call me Julie."

"Julie, I have some terrible news."

Diane tells Julie that Mike Davies is dead. The publisher is stunned. Both women remain quiet for some time until Julie lets out a long sigh.

"I just can't believe he's dead," she says. "Still, if I look at it from a business point of view, this is a blessing in disguise. This being his last book and published posthumously means its sales will surpass all projections!"

Although the publisher's commentary makes Diane cringe slightly, she has to agree. A dead author is like a dead painter – their works are more valuable once they pass away. Nevertheless, this is a murder, and solving it is more important than talking about sales figures.

"I liked the fellow though," says Julie. "He was a bit odd, remote really, but there was something quite endearing about him."

"Julie, there's more," says Diane. She explains that Mike has been killed under very suspicious circumstances, and whatever information Julie has about Mike and his manuscript might be most helpful to Detective Crothers.

"And you say he received the threats after he submitted the final draft to us?" Julie asks.

"Yes," Diane says. She does not tell the publisher that it appears the threatening letters were written on the publisher's stationary. Who knows? Julie Petrie could even be the author of the vile threats.

"Can you make it to Birmingham tomorrow? Why don't you come by my office so we can chat to see if I have anything helpful to offer? Say, 10am?"

"That's fine," says Diane. "I really should bring Detective Crothers with me, being his investigation and all. Is that alright with you?"

"See you both tomorrow morning. Goodnight Diane."

Not only should Darrell be there, but Diane would feel a lot safer with him there too. Knowing what she knows about the watermark on the threatening letters, the publishing house could be a danger zone. Now to somehow make sure the inspector can leave Lundy Island and make it to Birmingham for 10 tomorrow morning.

Diane takes out her wallet and pulls out a folded piece of paper that Sergeant Golden had given her. It has the number of the satellite phone that Golden has generously lent Darrell for the duration of his time on the island. It was mighty smart of Golden to do so and to share the number with Diane. She dials the number, hoping Darrell still has the phone with him.

"Inspector Darrell Crothers."

"Darrell, it's Diane."

"Diane, is everything alright?"

"Oh yes... fine... fine... is there any chance you can be in Birmingham tomorrow at 10 am?"

"Oh Diane... the forensic team has just arrived to finally process the yacht. They might be able to finish by tonight but..."

"I've arranged for us to meet the executive director at Mike's publisher's office."

"Isn't that a little premature?"

"Not if the threatening letters were written on the publisher's stationary."

"Diane!? Why didn't you say anything before?"

"I remembered it later and then when I did you were so busy organizing this and that..."

Diane tells the inspector that the threatening letters should be inside the cabin on the yacht, although she isn't sure where. Darrell pokes his head into the cabin and asks one of the forensic investigators if they came across any typed letters of a threatening nature. The investigator says they haven't, but that they are not finished processing the scene yet.

"The killer could have also taken them," Darrell and Diane say at the same time.

"But the cabin wasn't ransacked, and it didn't even appear to be rummaged through," says Diane.

Darrell then tells Diane that he's already talked to Dr. Jackson about his autopsy on Mike's body. He says a severe blow to the head, probably from a large rock or a similar type of object, was the cause of death. He says Golden and a couple of constables from the mainland are searching the area just to see if they can find a rock with any evidence on it.

"So Golden came back, did he?" Diane says jovially, while trying to ignore Darrell's statements about a 'large rock', 'blood' and ''hair.

"He did!" says Darrell. "I think he's found his footing."

The forensic investigator exits the yacht's cabin and joins the inspector on the pier. In his hands are two worn pieces of paper, each in their own evidence bag.

"Darrell? Are you still there?" Diane asks on the other end of the phone line.

"Just one moment Diane."

"Are these the letters you were after, sir?" the forensic investigator asks.

Darrell takes both in his hands and reads the small font, all caps, typed in the centre of each page. He reads the content to himself:

"DEAR MIKE DAVIES, KINDLY WITHDRAW YOUR LATEST MANUSCRIPT OR ELSE YOUR DAYS ARE NUMBERED."

and

"THIS IS YOUR LAST WARNING. CANCEL THE BOOK DEAL BEFORE IT'S TOO LATE FOR YOU."

He holds the letters up towards the setting sun and can faintly make out a watermark.

"Diane, can you tell me what you remember about the watermark on the threatening letters?"

"I remember a CP in cursive. CP stands for Copse Publishers."

"I'm going to catch the early morning ferry tomorrow and I'll meet you at the publisher's office at 10am."

"Oh, that's wonderful. Thank you Darrell... thank you."

When they hang up the phone, Darrell worries that he may be leaving the island too soon, but the forensic team appears to be almost finished. And Sergeant Golden is turning out to be an excellent second-in-command.

Speaking of Sergeant Golden, Darrell sees him practically sprinting towards him with the constables in tow. The mighty-but-limber police supervisor stops in front of the inspector. He's carrying a heavy object encased in an evidence bag and passes it to Darrell with inquiring eyes.

Darrell carefully handles the large piece of granite and scans it closely. He flips it over and sees a few roughly-ripped strands of white hair stuck to a sharp sliver of the rock – they're held in place by a reddish-brown substance. This could be Mike Davies' hair and blood.

"Well done Golden!" says Darrell, patting the sergeant enthusiastically on the back. "Where did you find it?"

"We searched the entire beach, sir," the Sergeant says, pointing to the rocky shore next to the pier.

"Most impressive!" beams Darrell. "Can I trust you to take this to the lab to test it for fingerprints and DNA?"

"Yes sir!" Golden practically shouts. He cannot hide his full-tooth smile.

Before passing the rock back to Golden, Darrell takes one last look. He wonders how many millions of years old this very piece of granite is and what stories it could tell from across the ages. Was this the very first murder it ever witnessed or played a role in?

Darrell cannot think about that now. He has to concentrate on making sure everything is organized before leaving the island. His biggest challenge perhaps is explaining to Mrs. Poole at the Puffin's Nest that he will not be staying long enough for the full breakfast she promised of poached eggs, griddle cakes, baked beans, grilled tomatoes and 'Old English' sausage.

Chapter 5

Diane finds a spot to park less than a five-minute walk away from Copse Publishers. She leaves the high-traffic road to find the pedestrian-only street where the boutique publisher is located.

The time is five minutes before 10, so most of Birmingham's workforce has already completed their Monday morning commute. Diane finds herself among mostly women, some with tots in tow, window shopping among the procession of independent and name-brand stores.

Diane spots Darrell heading towards a barista holding a tray of samples – some sort of espresso-based drink topped with whip cream – who is outside trying to drum up business for her café. By the looks of the bags under Darrell's eyes he could use several shots of strong espresso.

"You made good time!" Diane says to the inspector, while trying not to laugh at the whiff of whip cream stuck to his nostril. She pulls a napkin out of her purse and points to his nose.

"I got the island's conservationist to run me over to the mainland in his motorboat," says Darrell. "I didn't want to wait until this morning, so as soon as the forensics was done, he took me over last night."

Darrell had taken a brief nap in his car and then drove to Birmingham first thing this morning. Diane shakes her head like a concerned mum. For a moment she wonders whether she should have got her friend involved in this case. But who could do a better job than he?

"Well, we best go meet Mrs. Petrie," says Diane, pointing to the small "Copse Publishers" sign situated above another sign, one that reads "Ainslie Graphic Design." Both signs are bolted above a red doorway, tucked in between a shop selling bath and beauty products and a sushi restaurant.

They climb the stairs to the second floor to the publishing house. Darrell is a little surprised by the size of the office. As far as he can tell the entire space is three rooms at best; two offices and one reception room. It's definitely not as large as he expected it to be.

"Well, they are not a magazine or a newspaper publisher, pushing out a new issue every day or every month" whispers Diane. "They publish books, and only a few a year. And the actual printing happens in London."

"Newspapers? Do they still exist?" Darrell whispers with a smirk.

He then realizes it works to their advantage that Copse Publishers is smaller than he had anticipated. This means dealing with less potential "persons of interest"… it means the pool of people who had been technically allowed to read Mike Davies' manuscript is small.

Darrell suddenly realizes that he forgot to ask Dianne whether she told Mrs. Petrie about the threatening letters and how they were written on Copse Publishers' stationary.

As if she is reading the inspector's mind, Diane quickly whispers, "I did not tell her about the watermark on the pages of the threats."

She's told Darrell just in time as they hear footsteps from the back office coming out to meet them.

A short and spry woman dressed in a black pantsuit and pumps has come out to meet them. The skin tone facial concealer and her freshly-dyed, bright red hair do well to hide the marks she's developed over the 30 years she's spent working long hours in the publishing business.

"I'm Julie Petrie," she says, firmly shaking Diane's hand. "Diane, it's so nice to finally meet you face to face, even though the circumstances are not… the most comfortable."

She then introduces herself to the inspector. As she firmly shakes Darrell's hand too, he looks her straight in the eyes. The publisher does not flinch one bit.

"Thank you for taking the time to meet with us," says Darrell. "Is there somewhere we can sit and chat?"

Mrs. Petrie nods her head. She runs back to get her purse and invites Diane and the inspector to join her for a coffee at the café a few doors down. Once outside she tells them that it is perhaps better they speak outside the office.

"Since talking to you yesterday, Diane, it got me thinking," Mrs. Petrie whispers. "The walls might have ears, as they say."

Before Darrell or Diane can ask her if she suspects someone from the office in particular, Julie Petrie turns around and briskly walks towards the Java & Vanilla Bean Café. She swings open the purple-painted door that is bordered with painted images of multi-coloured mugs with steam rising above. Darrell jogs up to catch the door that Mrs. Petrie is holding open.

A young woman with dreadlocks tied into a bun and a sedate but genuine smile asks them if they would like anything to eat or drink. Julie orders a 'non-fat, extra-foam, extra-hot cappuccino in a large mug'; Diane and Darrell each order a cup of tea.

There are no customers in the café. They sit down at a small table, the one furthest from the counter. Diane and Darrell each take out a small notebook. They look at each other and nod their heads – it can't hurt for both of them to write down some pertinent details.

For a moment, Julie plays with the poetry magnets attached to a metal clipboard that is dangling just above their table; she then decides she'd better get on with it. She pulls her mobile out of her pocket and holds up the screen so only Darrell and Diane can see. She slowly swipes to show them pictures of four individuals, three women and one man. Each of them, knowingly posing for the camera, is clearly in an office environment at the time the pictures are taken. They are either sitting at a desk or beside a bookcase or a photocopier.

"Are these all of the employees who work for Copse Publishers?" Diane asks.

"Yes," says Julie. "And these are the people – the only people – who have read the hard copy of the manuscript."

"To your knowledge…" says Darrell, who stops short when the barista delivers their hot drinks to the table. When she leaves, Darrell asks, "Is it possible that anyone else has been in the office and accessed it?"

"I've been keeping the soft copy only on a flash drive, which I locked in the safe along with the hard copy," says Julie. "I checked again this morning and both are still locked up tight."

Julie explains that she asked each of her employees to read the hard copy and to give her their notes. As each borrowed the pages, she had them sign them out to make sure the manuscript was always accounted for.

"Is it possible that any one of them took the manuscript out to read at a restaurant or another public place during their lunch hour?" asks Diane.

"Oh it's possible, yes, but I would hope they wouldn't be daft enough to leave the pages out on a table, unsupervised. Oh God, I hope not," says Julie. "But the reason I brought you here, away from the office, is I have to tell you about one of my employees."

Julie holds up her phone and swipes back to the picture of Ingrid Bauer, who works as a copy editor but also does some online marketing for the small publishing house. Diane stares at the picture to see a woman, smiling yes, but with eyes that are not reciprocating.

Ingrid Bauer had told Julie that she tragically lost her father 25 years ago, right around the time of the fall of the Berlin Wall. Her father had been an East German soldier and had been in charge of guarding a British agent, an agent who had been captured on the East Berlin side of the Wall. The British agent was part of MI6. He then was successfully rescued, but during the extraction Ingrid's father was apparently killed.

"Ingrid said, 'The MI6 shot and killed my father. The MI6 are murderers!' She was quite emotional… understandably," recounts Julie.

"When did she tell you all of this?" asks Diane.

"Right after she read the manuscript," says Julie.

Diane and Darrell look at one another without saying a word. The inspector hates to jump to conclusions, but it looks like Ingrid Bauer has made it to the top of the suspect list. He will need to interview her as soon as possible. As for the other three individuals in Julie's photographs – the other Copse Publishers employees – they do not appear to have any particular personal interest in Mike Davies' story. But as we all know, appearances can be very deceiving, and Darrell should interview all of the publishing house personnel, including a formal interview with Julie Petrie. But first he has to make an appearance at the station in Shrewsbury. He is due to see the superintendent this afternoon.

Diane and Darrell thank Julie for meeting with them and leave her to finish her especially foamy cappuccino.

"Diane, do you mind walking me to my car?" Darrell asks, as they leave the Java & Vanilla Bean.

Diane looks around at the casual pedestrians and shopkeepers in a jocular fashion. "Are you wanting me to protect you from this suspicious crowd?" she says in jest.

"Hardy har har… I just want to run something by you," says the detective.

Darrell opens the boot of his Range Rover and climbs in. Diane stares after him, amused, wondering what he's up to. Then she sees a small safe pushed against the back seat and Darrell is punching in the security code to open it.

"You can never be too careful…" says Diane.

"Ever since my wife's car was broken into last year, I thought I better get a safe. All the robbers took was some footie equipment, but I kept thinking what if it had been my car and they had gotten their hands on some police evidence… or my lucky fishing lures," Darrell winks.

The inspector passes Diane some pages held in evidence bags. She's seen these before, and not too long ago: "DEAR MIKE DAVIES, KINDLY WITHDRAW YOUR LATEST MANUSCRIPT OR ELSE YOUR DAYS ARE NUMBERED" and "THIS IS YOUR

LAST WARNING. CANCEL THE BOOK DEAL BEFORE IT'S TOO LATE FOR YOU."

"Can you confirm with one hundred percent certainty that these are typed on Copse Publishers' stationary?" Darrell asks.

"If you had asked me this morning at quarter to 10, I would have said yes, but with 95 percent certainty. You see, I think I must have recycled the hard copy letters Julie Petrie had sent me using her company's stationary. They were basically generic monthly newsletters sent out to a mailing list. Our main correspondence, Julie's and mine, specifically about Mike's book, had been through e-mail," Diane says. "But now I can say with absolute certainty that these letters have the Copse Publishers' watermark."

Diane pulls out a folded piece of paper from her pocket. She unfolds it and holds it next to the letters encased in the evidence bags. Just to be sure she holds all of them up to the sun to reveal the cursive *CP* symbols at the bottom of each page.

"I nicked the page from a pile on the front desk when Julie ran to get her purse," beams Diane.

"You little devil!" Darrell laughs. "I'll be in touch soon. Try to get some rest, will ya?"

Diane leaves the inspector so he can get on his way to Shrewsbury. Before heading back to Apple Mews, she decides to walk back to the Java & Vanilla Bean – she'd quite like to try one of those foamy cappuccinos herself.

Whilst thinking about Ingrid Bauer, Diane almost walks right into a mom pushing a double pram with a baby and tot inside; and again almost into a greyhound and his owner. But Diane cannot help thinking about the section of Mike's book that must have entirely floored Ingrid.

How Mike described the rescue of the MI6 agent was so vivid, and it did include an East German soldier being fatally shot. The level of detail, the emotion his phrases carried, made Diane feel that this had actually happened, and that Mike had not only witnessed the course of events, but had also been deeply affected by them. Diane had not dared ask him how accurate the depiction was nor did she inquire about what role he played. She was positive Mike hadn't been the captive, but perhaps he had been part of the team that rescued the agent. Maybe Ingrid Bauer thought so too – maybe she even thought Mike Davies had been the one that pulled the trigger and killed her father.

Passing by the window of the café, Diane sees that Julie is no longer sitting at the round table far from the counter. She re-enters the purple door and joins the queue inside the now busier Java & Vanilla Bean.

After pulling out her wallet, Diane looks to the front of the line and sees a slender woman, perhaps 40 years of age, with slightly dishevelled, sandy blond hair. Diane swears she looks similar to one of the photos she'd just seen on Julie's mobile phone.

"Are you having a dark roast today, Ingrid?" asks the barista with the dreadlocked hair.

Diane drops her wallet on the floor. Her clumsiness due to being caught off guard has made a noise so loud that everyone in the café, including Ingrid, looks her way. Diane quickly picks the wallet up, looks in Ingrid's eyes for a brief moment, and scurries out of the café.

"I think I'll have a cuppa when I get home," Diane says under her breath, and she hurries towards her car.

When Darrell arrives at the Shrewsbury Police Station, he finds the superintendent sitting at Darrell's desk.

Darrell has great respect for Superintendent Ian Groves, a superior who can be stern when he needed to be, but who is always fair. When he sees Darrell, he shoots him a warm but serious smile.

"You've covered a lot of territory the last couple days, Crothers," says the superintendent in his husky voice.

"Yes, sir."

"As you know, I have no objection to the work you're doing – we haven't had much to worry about around here lately, so I like to share resources when we can."

"Thank you, sir."

The superintendent tells him that there is someone here who wants to talk to "Inspector Crothers" especially. All that he's told Superintendent Groves is that he's Agent Somerset from MI6.

"I can't say I'm surprised, based on what you've told me about your murder victim's work history," says the superintendent.

Darrell can't help but smile. The grapevine, in instances such as these, works faster than emails or text messages. Still, is it a tad disconcerting that an agency like the MI6 would still be keeping such active tabs on their retired agents?

The superintendent leads Darrell into his office and shuts the door. Agent Somerset stands when they come in.

"Agent Somerset, this is Inspector Crothers."

The two men shake hands but neither sits. The superintendent walks around the desk to sit in his own chair, and with a determined look, urges Darrell to do the same. The agent follows suit but only after he begins to talk.

"I am aware of Mike Davies' sudden death, and I'm sure you have already uncovered that he was a retired MI6 agent," he says.

The superintendent and Darrell nod, and Darrell says, "May I ask how you came to know about his death... and this inquiry?"

Agent Somerset ignores Darrell's question and says, "It is probably some vandals living on or around the island who are responsible."

"With all due respect," says Darrell, "the evidence we've retrieved so far doesn't really point to the work of vandals. We have to explore all motives and all possible suspects."

"May I remind you that Lundy Island does not fall under your jurisdiction," says Agent Somerset. "And in the grand scheme, the Shrewsbury Police rank low within Britain's chain of command."

"Are you trying to scare me? Stop me from investigating this murder?"

"I'm trying to do what's best for Great Britain," says the agent in a pretentious tone. "And let me make myself clear, the British government does not want something from twenty-five years ago to come out of the shadows to be scrutinized."

Before Darrell can say another word, Superintendent Groves quickly stands and thanks the agent for coming in. "Duly noted," the superintendent says, shaking Agent Somerset's hand.

Darrell knows that the superintendent and he have to bow to the powers-that-be, but he can't help thinking the MI6 has just a little too much power in this instance. A murderer will go free if he is not able to proceed with this investigation, and why? Is it because the MI6 is afraid of looking bad? Or is there more to it than that?

When Superintendent Groves returns from seeing the agent out, he shuts the door anticipating a loud reaction from Darrell.

"In all my 15 years as a detective, I have never been asked to *not* investigate any crime, let alone a homicide!" Darrell yells.

He tells the superintendent about how the threatening letters that Mike received were typed on Copse Publishers' stationary, and how an employee at the publisher's office, Ingrid Bauer, is a viable suspect. The fact that a scene in the book strongly mirrors what actually happened to her father could very well have incited her to commit a murder. And now because the MI6 wants to cover up an old story, she is to remain free?

"Do you think that this Ingrid Bauer thought Mike Davies made light of what happened twenty-five years ago and that angered her?" asks Superintendent Groves. "Or do you think this angered someone in the MI6?"

The two men sit and ponder this for a while. Was it that Mike made light of that event or did he share too many details about what happened? One thing is for sure – if his book is the motive of his murder, he certainly paid for writing about that time in history with his life.

"I need to at least interview Ingrid Bauer, sir?"

"I'm inclined to agree with you Darrell," says the superintendent. "I don't like the idea of a murderer going free either, just because the MI6 decides they don't want their skeletons to fall out of the closet."

Superintendent Groves tells Darrell that he will talk to his own superiors immediately and get to the bottom of this – to find out whom, from on high, is calling the shots about the murder investigation of Mike Davies.

Chapter 6

Upset and frustrated from his meeting with Agent Somerset, Darrell needs to blow off some steam. Although for a brief moment he is tempted to blow off everything and go far away to some fishing cabin in Scotland, or even Canada for that matter, he quickly decides he is not going to give up. MI6 or no MI6, Mike Davies deserves justice.

Darrell calls his wife Claire to tell her he's going to visit Diane Dimbleby before going home. Claire can sense the strain in her husband's voice and she's grateful he's found someone he can talk to when times get tough, as she knows a role in law enforcement often does get challenging emotionally, not that Darrell would ever admit this. Before his mum had passed away she had been a great comfort to her son. It seems Darrell has a similar bond with Diane, except that she also seems to like to get quite involved with investigating murders – something Darrell's mum did not like so much.

When Darrell arrives at Diane's Apple Mews home, she, as always, is not surprised. She's made an extra large pot of tikka masala, and anticipating the inspector might stop by, she's added more chicken than she might normally – she usually adds as many or more carrots and beans as chicken to the mix.

"You're just in time to have some chicken and veg masala," says Diane, opening the door.

"I'm sorry for not calling first," Darrell says almost meekly.

"No need to call first, my friend," says Diane. "If you don't mind me saying so, you look as if you've just been in a boxing match, although there is no clear sign of who won."

"Well, you're not far off," says Darrell, managing to crack a small smile.

Sitting down at the table, while they tuck into the deliciously spicy dish, Rufus does a good job of calming Darrell down and even cheering him up. The dog cannot seem to get enough of the inspector's attention. Rufus has quickly realized that he loves to lie across Darrell's feet. When his deep breaths become louder and louder snores, Darrell for a time forgets about how angry and frustrated he is, and bursts into laughter.

"I think you make Rufus very comfortable... literally and figuratively," smiles Diane.

When Darrell's laughter subsides, he tells Diane about the meeting he had with his superintendent and the MI6 agent, Agent Somerset.

"He basically had the gall to tell me not to carry on with the investigation. He said the British government does not want events from twenty-five years ago to be public knowledge..."

"Has Agent Somerset read Mike's book?" Diane asks.

The question catches Darrell off guard; he hadn't thought of that. He has no idea whether the agent would have read the manuscript, but how could he of? Well, he is a spy so he must have his ways...

It would make sense that Agent Somerset read the manuscript, since he was hinting about not wanting the events that happened twenty-five years ago in Berlin – events that inspired Mike's novel – to come to light.

"Do you think he did?" asks Darrell.

"Well, if this Agent Somerset knows about the book and its contents, he could have been the one who decided to eliminate Mike, with the MI6's blessing of course," Diane says.

Darrell shudders. Would the MI6 actually kill one of their own? Still, he agrees that it is an avenue worth exploring. Being in a room with Agent Somerset again could potentially make the inspector's blood boil. Darrell would have to make sure to mentally prepare for that interview, so he wouldn't let his anger flare up again, although it rarely did.

"Well, if Somerset or any of his fellow agents had something to do with Mike's death, it makes sense that he told me that the highest authorities do not approve of me investigating," says Darrell. "It's the perfect cover. For all we know, his superiors might not even know about Mike Davies."

Diane suddenly has a flashback to a time before Mike had even joined the MI6.

"He must have been barely 18," Diane tells Darrell. "My family was visiting with his in London. Mike had joined the army and was going off to the academy for training in a few days. His mother made him try on his uniform for us. When he came out in his camouflage and cap, I remember he was blushing. He wasn't ashamed I don't think, just unsure. It was always expected he would join up just like his dad. He was perfectly capable – both athletic and intelligent. I do remember him admitting to me though that he was scared. Of course he did fine, so fine that he was a top choice when the MI6 was recruiting."

Darrell's mobile phone rings. He apologizes to Diane, but he has to pick it up – it's his superintendent calling. Superintendent Groves says he's sending a female officer to spend the night at Diane's home. He's just got off the phone with a friend in London who knows a little more about the ins-and-outs of government agencies.

"Your friend is in serious danger," says the superintendent.

"Diane? Are you sure? Why?" Darrell asks.

"Well, let's just say the MI6 might stop at nothing to eliminate any possible *witness*, someone privy to an event that might make the agency vulnerable... an event like in Germany, twenty-five years ago," says the superintendent. "They do not want to compromise their security... their secrecy... their integrity."

Darrell is beyond surprised that Diane has been identified by the superintendent's 'intel' as a serious target. Sure, Darrell himself had been worried about her when they were on Lundy Island, so close to where the murder happened. But surely her life isn't at risk while she's in her very own Apple Mews... at least her life shouldn't be at risk *again*. Like they say, "lightning never strikes the same place twice" – or is that just a myth?

"Do you really think MI6 would kill an innocent civilian, superintendent?" asks Darrell "I mean it's plain barmy! And besides, wouldn't the five people who work at Copse Publishers also be on their... kill list... too?"

"I know it sounds ludicrous," says Superintendent Groves. "But until I speak to the top brass in London tomorrow morning, and find out who is in charge and who is actually a threat, I want to make sure Mrs. Dimbleby is safe. Besides, her life has been threatened more than once during... *ahem*... several other murder investigations."

The superintendent is right. How can Darrell even question the presence of an officer keeping an eye on Diane? He vividly remembers the time she was kidnapped and could have been easily killed, and the time that dreadful Mrs. Rosalyn Thomas and her son broke into her house to take her down. It's amazing that this brave woman is still willing to be Darrell's confidant and fellow sleuth.

They hear a knock at the door.

"That'll be the officer that's coming to stay the night," says Darrell, opening the door. "Hello Shannon, thank you for coming."

Darrell introduces Diane to Constable Shannon Toft. While Diane does not feel she needs the extra attention, she's happy for the company. The inspector takes his leave and Diane puts on the kettle so the two women can share a cuppa before Diane and Rufus head up to bed.

While Diane sleeps soundly for the first time since Mike Davies was killed, Darrell does not sleep a wink. But he hasn't been tossing and turning in bed next to his wife – the inspector has intentionally stayed awake.

After leaving Diane's place the night before, Darrell headed to Birmingham. More specifically, he drove to a street with a series of three to five-storey apartment buildings. Inside one of these buildings is the flat that Ingrid Bauer calls home. Darrell is parked across the street from said building and has successfully managed to stay awake. It hadn't been an easy task, since the cumulative lack of sleep has been catching up with him. To keep from dozing off he consciously tried to think of highlights of his children's lives from every year they've been alive.

Darrell had no problem thinking of examples – their first steps, holidays and fishing excursions, Chloe scoring her first goal, Jeremy winning an art contest – but it had been a little difficult to figure out how old they were when certain events happened. He had to stop himself from calling Claire a couple times to say, "Do you remember when…." He's sure she would have liked to share these memories with him – just not at three o'clock in the morning.

But now it's just a few minutes after six and the first sunrays are shining through his Range Rover's windshield. Darrell is starting to wonder if he's wasting his time. It's probable that like most people, Ingrid Bauer sleeps at night. Why did he think he'd catch her sneaking away from her apartment in the middle of the night? And for what reason? If she had killed Mike Davies, there isn't anything for her to clean up in Birmingham... or is there?

Still Darrell decides he'll stay until 8:30 or 9, when Ingrid might be more likely to head out, possibly even to the publisher's office.

Darrell's determination is slightly rewarded. To his sheer luck, he sees a man unlock the little news stall that's on the pavement just a few metres away. By the looks of a poster on the side of the stall, it looks the small business not only sells newspapers and magazines, but also coffee and tea. Darrell would even settle for a lukewarm beverage at this point.

He gives the owner a few minutes to get settled before heading over to see if he's able to purchase a small bit of comfort in a Styrofoam cup, all the while keeping an eye on Ingrid Bauer's building's main entrance.

"I don't suppose you have any coffee brewing?" Darrell asks.

"I do," says the short, thick side-burned man, who looks to be around Darrell's age. "By the looks of it, you could use a whole pot!"

"How about we start with a cup," Darrell laughs.

"I saw you in your car when I got here. Were you waiting for me to open? I didn't think my coffee was that good," the gentleman laughs.

"Truth be told, I'm doing some surveillance," a tired Darrell says somewhat recklessly.

"Not on me, I hope," the stall owner laughs.

"No," laughs Darrell. "But just to warn you, I'll be here for a few more hours."

"I'll keep the coffee coming then," the man smiles.

"Ta," says Darrell, pouring more sugar and cream into his cup than usual.

Sitting in the driver's seat and devouring the hot newsstand coffee, Darrell gets a second wind, or perhaps a third or a fourth. He's staring intently at the people in business suits and casual dress, and the mums or dads with their kids in school uniforms, rushing out the door of Ingrid Bauer's building. He quickly looks at his watch to realize it's already a few minutes after 8 am. Just as Darrell takes out his mobile, about to ring Claire to see how she and the kids are getting on, somebody knocks on the passenger door window. It's the newsstand owner – bless him, he's carrying another cup of coffee. Darrell lowers the window.

"This is on the house," says the newsstand man. "It's not every day I can show my appreciation to a copper!"

"Ta," smiles Darrell.

"There's something I've been wondering if I should tell ya," says the man.

"Go on," says Darrell.

He tells the inspector about how yesterday, a car had been parked in the very spot where Darrell is now, for several hours. He remembers it well because it was a BMW Series 4 Gran Coupé, and cars like that seldom make an appearance in this neighbourhood. The windows were tinted, and since he thought no one was in the car, the newsstand man took a couple pictures with his phone – he was going to show them to his son, who loves cars.

"Well, as soon I started taking pictures, someone got out of the car and started yelling at me."

"What did he look like?" asks Darrell.

"He was tall, about your height, brown hair… he had on a suit and some sunglasses. After I told him I was just going to show the photos to my son, he still made me delete them. He then got back in the car and stayed for another hour…"

"Thank you for telling me," says Darrell.

There could be a thousand explanations as to who the man in the BMW was and what he was doing parked here for so long. For all Darrell knows, the mystery man could have been pulled over to have a lengthy chat on his mobile with his mum. But is there a possibility it could have been MI6?

Just as the inspector starts to wonder again whether he's wasting his time, just sitting here waiting for perhaps *nothing* that will help solve the case, his mobile starts to ring. It's his superintendent calling.

Darrell picks up and learns the most unexpected… the most startling… the most eerie news – eerie because he's so physically close to the person and place for which the superintendent is calling about. Superintendent Groves has just said, "Ingrid Bauer is dead."

A neighbour had found her body. Apparently, the neighbour heard Ingrid's cat meowing, which wasn't out of the ordinary except that this morning it had been so loud that it caused the neighbour to be concerned. She opened Ingrid's front door – which by chance happened to be unlocked – after knocking for several minutes. It doesn't necessarily matter how or why the neighbour found Ingrid dead, unless Ingrid died by foul play, and if that was the case, the neighbour's story would have to be questioned and analysed.

But Darrell isn't thinking about all of this… yet. He takes in a deep breath and, for some reason, his first thought is that the MI6 definitely has something to hide.

Superintendent Groves tells Darrell that police have been dispatched to the scene. Darrell decides he better wait for them to arrive before going into the apartment himself.

When the Birmingham police cruiser arrives, Darrell walks over and introduces himself to the constables. He briefly explains that Ingrid Bauer, the person who is presumably dead, is involved in a case he is currently working on. The officers voice no objection and in fact take the senior officer's lead in approaching the apartment.

They walk into the lobby, and Darrell and the constables show the concierge their ID. Darrell tells him they've been called to investigate Ingrid Bauer's apartment and the concierge obligingly takes them up in the elevator to the third floor. The concierge is all set to let them into her flat, except they find that her front door is already wide open.

"Thank you for taking us up here," says Darrell to the concierge. "We'll take it from here."

The concierge hesitantly returns to the elevator, while Darrell and the constables slowly walk inside the flat. In the room closest to the door, they see a young woman, clearly in shock, sitting in a chair next to a body lying on the floor. The young woman is almost certainly the neighbour, and the body is almost certainly Ingrid Bauer.

Although Darrell has thought about Ingrid Bauer almost constantly for the last 24 hours, he suddenly realizes that he has never actually met the woman in the flesh.

Now he's staring down at her – someone still too young to have left this world – and clearly sees the bullet wound in her head and the gun lying next to her side. Without saying a word, the woman in shock stands and passes Darrell a piece of paper.

Before he even reads the words on the page, Darrell finds himself looking for any distinctive watermark on the piece of paper, but does not find any. In typewritten font, the note reads,

"NOW THAT MY FATHER'S KILLER IS ELIMINATED, I'VE NOTHING ELSE TO LIVE FOR.

SINCERELY, INGRID BAUER"

This sounds like a suicide note and a confession all in one.

Darrell notices in the corner of the room, a desk with both a laptop and a printer – this could have been where the letter was produced.

'Now that my father's killer is eliminated...' This must mean that Ingrid believed Mike Davies had killed her father *(had Mike killed her father?)*. So she must have avenged her father's death... but in the letter she does

not necessarily admit that she killed Mike Davies, did she?

Darrell slowly walks over to the desk. Ingrid's computer has gone to sleep but the printer is still turned on. He puts on a pair of gloves and presses a random key on the keyboard. The laptop screen comes to life to reveal an open word processing document. The text cursor is blinking next to the end of the typed note, next to the words 'SINCERELY, INGRID BAUER.'

Darrell opens the top drawer of the desk and spots a notebook. He picks up the notebook and flips to the last handwritten entry. Skimming the previous entries, common phrases jump out: *'The British government is to blame'* and *'the MI6 killed my father'*…

When she hears the phone ringing, Diane quickly runs inside from the backyard, where she and Constable Shannon Toft are playing catch with Rufus.

"Hello?!"

"Diane, quick, turn on BBC Radio 4!" shouts Albert over the phone.

Diane knows her friend and if he is taking the time to call her to tell her to listen to something on the radio, there must be a good reason. Without hanging up, she runs over to the radio that is sitting on the kitchen counter – it's already tuned to BBC Radio 4.

"ACCORDING TO A PRESS RELEASE PROVIDED BY JULIE PETRIE OF COPSE PUBLISHERS, THE FICTION BOOK THAT HER COMPANY WILL PUBLISH NEXT MONTH IS INSPIRED BY MIKE DAVIES' TIME WITH THE SECRET INTELLIGENCE SERVICE. PETRIE SUGGESTS THAT THE DEATH OF DAVIES MAY BE CONNECTED TO HIS BOOK; SHE ALSO STATES THAT INGRID BAUER, DECEASED, WHOSE BODY WAS FOUND THIS MORNING, ALSO HAD A CONNECTION TO DETAILS IN DAVIES' STORY. POLICE HAVE NOT YET REVEALED THE CAUSE OF BAUER'S DEATH, ALTHOUGH A WITNESS, WHO HAS ASKED NOT TO BE NAMED, SAYS BAUER TOOK HER OWN LIFE… IN OTHER NEWS…"

"Oh my goodness! Ingrid Bauer is dead!?" Diane gasps.

"So it *is* your friend Mike they are talking about then?" Albert asks with an empathetic tone.

"Yes… thank you for calling Albert. I had no idea of this latest development."

"Diane, are you quite alright?"

"I've had a constable here with me overnight, so I'm being protected, but I don't think I'm in the line of fire," Diane says, mustering a little laugh.

"See you tomorrow?"

"Yes, tomorrow Albert, although I haven't gotten much writing done to share with you," says Diane.

"My dear, you and you alone are more than enough to make an old man like me happy," Albert chuckles.

When the two friends hang up, Diane calls Rufus in for his supper. Constable Toft follows the dog inside. Her smile quickly morphs into a look of concern when she sees Diane's overwhelmed expression.

Before the constable has time to ask Diane what's wrong, there's a knock at the door. Diane starts to go towards it, but is quickly stopped by Constable Toft who insists on answering it instead.

To both Diane and Constable Toft's relief, it is Inspector Darrell Crothers standing on the other side of the front door. He thanks the constable for pulling the overtime and sends her home, but not before Diane insists the officer take home some muffins just baked that morning.

When Diane and Darrell are each settled on the couch with a glass of wine in hand, she tells him about what she heard on the radio.

"I heard the same story on another station while driving here," says Darrell. "And the superintendent says it's on the tele too. By nightfall, all of the UK will be aware of Mike Davies and Ingrid Bauer and MI6's cover-up."

"Julie Petrie really wants to milk these tragedies as much as she can all in the name of book sales, although I'm proud of my friend, Mike, and his book," says Diane. "But I still can't believe Julie Petrie went to the press so quickly after Ingrid Bauer took her own life."

"If she did take her own life," says Darrell quietly.

"You don't think it's a suicide?"

Darrell says that they still do not have the full medical examiner's report, and he isn't completely convinced that MI6 might not have something to do with her death. The suicide note had been typed, and it was not even signed, so anyone could have written it. Plus he had seen several people go in and out of Ingrid Bauer's building throughout the night. While none of them stood out, who knows if one of them shot Ingrid?

"The one advantage of Julie Petrie going public," Darrell says, "is that your life is no longer in danger. What Mike wrote about, about his and MI6's time during the fall of the Berlin Wall, is no longer a secret."

Darrell's mobile rings. He looks and sees that it is Dr. Jackson who is calling. He, *again*, through more coaxing and promises of breakfasts along with packed lunches, had convinced the medical examiner to do one 'last' favour and go to Birmingham to examine the body of Ingrid Bauer. Dr. Jackson says he isn't finished with the examination yet, but wanted to let Darrell know that no gunshot residue was found on Ingrid's hands.

As the doctor explains though, this does not rule out suicide. Apparently, those who fire a gun do not necessarily test positive for GSR in one hundred percent of cases. And unfortunately, Dr. Jackson discovered that before he arrived in Birmingham, fingernail scrapings were mistakenly taken before GSR samples were gathered. This means if Ingrid Bauer did have gunshot residue on her hands, it could have been wiped away.

When he hangs up the phone with the medical examiner, Darrell tells Diane the latest development.

"So let's imagine Ingrid Bauer did not kill herself... do we then think MI6 did?" Diane posits.

"At least a part of me imagines they could be responsible, "says Darrell.

"Did you ever find any evidence on the rock that was found at Lundy, the possible murder weapon that killed Mike?" asks Diane.

"We confirmed the hair and blood to be Mike's, but we found no fingerprints and no DNA belonging to anybody else," Darrell explains.

"So who had a greater motive to kill Mike? Ingrid with her anger, or the MI6 and their need for discretion?" says Diane.

"We might never know," says Darrell.

Diane changes the subject and tells Darrell her plans on how to pay tribute to her friend. She has already started working on a eulogy to read at his funeral. She wants to remind everyone of his loyalty and his desire for transparency and justice for all.

Since Mike had requested that he be cremated when he died, Diane came up with an idea. She is going to arrange for some of their mutual friends to take a bit of his ashes with them on their travels. His dream had been to sail around the world on his yacht, so at least this way he would still get to cover a lot of distance and be brought to various parts of the world.

"We should say a toast for your friend," says Darrell, raising his glass.

Diane smiles and says, "Keep them straight, Mike!"

He may have risked his life writing this last book, Diane thinks, but he did it because he really did believe in justice for all.

♠ ♠ ♠ ♠ ♠ ♠

In Mauerpark in Berlin, a young teen is juggling a football masterfully with his feet. Fully focused on the ball, he rams right into someone and falls to the ground. Disoriented for just a moment, the boy reopens his eyes to see the person who he must have collided into already a number of strides away. He watches after the person who is clothed in a dark hood and long coat. The teen stands up and finds himself following behind at a safe distance. He's not sure why he's following, but feels compelled to do so.

After about five minutes of walking, the teen sees the person stop and stand very still next to a remaining piece of the former Berlin Wall. The person kneels and slowly puts something down on the ground. After a long pause, the person continues on his or her way.

The teen, now very curious, quickly walks to the spot next to the graffitied section of wall where the person had paused. The teen is too young to remember the Berlin Wall properly, but has been told by his parents of the city's former state of division.

The boy picks up the item off the ground that the hooded person had left behind. The teen can immediately tell by its shape and its passport-sized photo that it is an identification card. He knows enough English to be able to read at the top of the ID:

"SECRET   INTELLIGENCE   SERVICE   – MICHAEL DAVIES."

Get Your Free Copy of
"Murder at the Inn"

Don't forget to grab your free copy of Penelope Sotheby's first novella *Murder At The Inn* while you still can.

Go to http://fantasticfiction.info/murder-at-the-inn/ to find out more.

Other Books By This Author

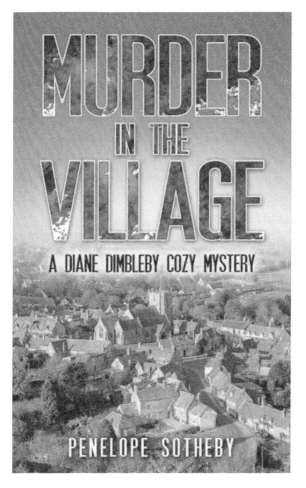

Murder in the Village

"Albert was completing his second full rotation in an effort to find something weapon-like when he heard a thud downstairs, followed by the sound of falling pottery. He stopped his spinning and wandered to the door, ready to peer out and ask about the noise. There was a commotion on the staircase and a form appeared in the bedroom doorway.

"Well, it looks like the time for subtlety is over," said the murderer as they raised a long sharp knife from their side."

The Apple Mews Centennial Fête is right around the corner and the locals are busy preparing for the big day. Quirky personalities abound as tables and tents are set up on the green, and now everyone is waiting to hear the results of the hotly debated baking contest. All is dandy until a murder during the festivities plunges Diane Dimbleby and Inspector Darrell Crothers together in yet another mystery.

The retired teacher-turned-author knew the baking competition this year was especially fierce, but would one of the participants really kill to win? It appears so. Just as the reigning champion is celebrating a record-breaking victory, she collapses. Diane finds clues and suspects galore in her quaint, picturesque town, but another contestant is murdered in the meantime. It turns out the victims had a dark secret they were hiding, and Diane and Inspector Crothers believe someone familiar--someone from the village--is responsible for their deaths.

Apple Mews is supposed to be peaceful. You should be able to trust your neighbors. Diane is tasked with her most personal case to date and it looks like timing is running out to save the next victims.

A curious writer. A determined detective. Too many suspects and not enough evidence. Murder at the Fête: A Diane Dimbleby Cozy Mystery is the fourth in the Diane Dimbleby series of books by author Penelope Sotheby.

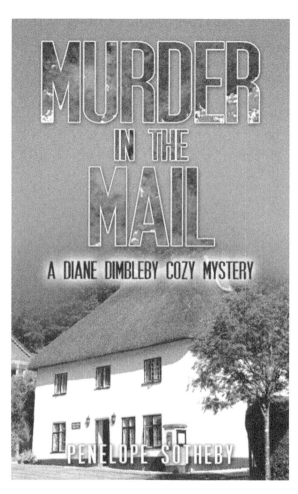

Murder in the Mail

"Inspector! Finally, I have gotten through to you. This is urgent. I know who the killer is, and you need to hurry. He has another girl!" Diane's words tumbled out of her in her haste to get the information where it could do some good.

"What? How?" said the Inspector.

"That's completely the wrong question right now, Inspector. Who? Who is the question of the moment. And the who is called......"

The village of Apple Mews is known for its old-world charm and friendly neighbors. No crime to speak of, except for a few startling occurrences during the past year. Now things have finally settled, and everyone is enjoying the safe haven they've always known and loved. However, when a traumatized girl from a nearby town appears on her doorstep, mystery author Diane Dimbleby is knee-deep in the middle of another whodunit.

Monica Hope doesn't have any enemies that she knows of, so she frantically reaches out to Diane after receiving a macabre package that contains a bejeweled severed finger. Inspector Darrel Crothers is called in and Diane hopes that together, with his experience and her uncanny sleuthing, they can solve this new inquest easily, but only if they work quickly. The inspector is dealing with personal demons of his own--struggling a demanding career with a patient, yet lonely wife--and he's a bit distracted; therefore, Diane calls on a longtime friend for a favor.

The investigation leads Diane to a local jeweler, who helps identify the exquisite ring on the deceased's finger. But a case of mistaken identity catapults the case in a direction Diane never saw coming. Clues are beginning to add up, and so are potential suspects. Can Diane and Darrell catch the killer before they strike again?

A curious writer. A determined detective. A not-so-special delivery. Murder in the Mail: A Diane Dimbleby Cozy Mystery is the fifth in the Diane Dimbleby series of books by author Penelope Sotheby.

Murder in the Development

"Diane looked at her notes and tried to let Albert's brightening spirits lift her own. She tried. A darkness sat heavily upon them, however, and the more Diane considered the possibilities, the more leaden her spirits became. There was a wicked person on the loose and, if the anger shown in the house was any indicator, the Carstairs may be in serious danger. And as the protectors of Monique, she and Albert may have brought that evil straight to their own door."

Diane gets a surprise visit one day from a young woman called Monique. Monique's husband Jonathan has gone missing and so she wants Diane to help find out what happened. Monique suspects foul play – especially as their luxury house has been vandalized and the word "Traitor" daubed in red paint on the window.

It isn't long before Diane finds out that Johnathan had made several enemies as a result of his job as an accountant. Did anyone hate Johnathan enough though to commit murder? That is what Diane must find out because if somebody killed Johnathan, they would certainly have no hesitation in killing again in order to cover it up.

A curious writer. A determined detective. A missing man. Murder in the Development: A Diane Dimbleby Cozy Mystery is the sixth in the Diane Dimbleby series of books by author Penelope Sotheby.

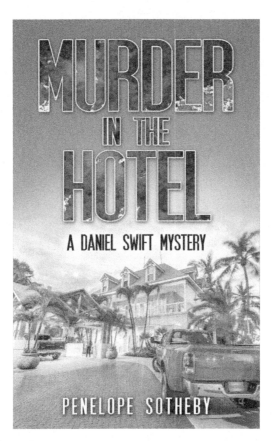

Murder in the Hotel

"Bill Levy," he said, taking Bill by the arms and putting on some handcuffs. "You are under arrest for the murder of Sean Harpo. You have the right to remain silent. Anything you say can and will be used against you. You have the right to an attorney. If you cannot afford an attorney one will be appointed for you. Do you have any questions about these rights as I have explained them to you?"

"No sir," Detective Barclay turned Bill around and started to walk him out of the room. He stopped and gave Daniel a wink and a wicked smile. "You have a nice day now," he said before leaving the hotel room.

"Don't worry, and don't say anything Bill," Daniel called after him. "I'll find out where they are taking you and be there quickly."

Daniel told Lindsay to stay put. "Everything said in the room stays between us, got it? There is something fishy going on here."

Daniel Swift - Attorney at Law. Honest. Dedicated. Brilliant. Together with his investigator friend, Jason Hunter, and his loyal clerk and assistant Kristie Starr, they make sure that justice is served in the Florida Keys. When Daniel gets a visit from Lindsay Gill, asking for help in getting her fiancé released from a Sanitarium, it triggers a chain of events which culminate in murder!!

About The Author

For many, the thought of childhood conjures images of hopscotch games in quiet neighbourhoods, and sticky visits to the local sweet shop. For Penelope Sotheby, childhood meant bathing in Bermuda, jiving in Jamaica and exploring a string of strange and exotic British territories with her nomadic family. New friends would come and go, but her constant companion was an old, battered collection of Agatha Christie novels that filled her hours with intrigue and wonder.

Penelope would go on to read every single one of Christie's sixty-six novels—multiple times—and so was born a love of suspense than can be found in Sotheby's own works today.

In 2011 the author debuted with *"Murder at the Inn"*, a whodunit novella set on Graham Island off the West Coast of Canada. After receiving positive acclaim, Sotheby went on to write the series *"Murder in Paradise"*; five novels following the antics of a wedding planner navigating nuptials (and crime scenes) in the tropical locations of Sotheby's formative years.

An avid gardener, proud mother, and passionate host of Murder Mystery weekends, Sotheby can often be found at her large oak table, gleefully plotting the demise of her friends, tricky twists and grand reveals.

Fantastic Fiction

Fantastic Fiction publishes short reads that feature stories in a series of five or more books. Specializing in genres such as Mystery, Thriller, Fantasy and Sci Fi, our novels are exciting and put our readers at the edge of their seats.

Each of our novellas range around 20,000 words each and are perfect for short afternoon reads. Most of the stories published through Fantastic Fiction are escapist fiction and allow readers to indulge in their imagination through well written, powerful and descriptive stories.

Why Fiction?

At Fantastic Fiction, we believe that life doesn't get much better than kicking back and reading a gripping piece of fiction. We are passionate about supporting independent writers and believe that the world should have access to this incredible works of fiction. Through our store we provide a diverse range of fiction that is sure to satisfy.

www.fantasticfiction.info

Made in the USA
Coppell, TX
25 March 2023

14744970R00184